AMISH BLISS

BOOK 10 THE AMISH BONNET SISTERS

SAMANTHA PRICE

CHAPTER 1

Florence held her baby daughter against her shoulder and stared out the window of her small cottage watching the sun rise. Carter was still upstairs asleep and, barely able to keep her eyes open, Florence wanted nothing more than a little extra sleep herself. They'd both woken during the night, taking it in turns to calm their baby who wasn't a good sleeper.

As she did most mornings, Florence stood on tippy toes to glimpse the next-door orchard. There wasn't much to see except for the treetops. She'd heard from the girls that Levi was doing better with managing it. He'd even pruned the trees with the help of her half-sisters and she hoped they did it well. A certain amount of knowledge was needed. Each plant was an individual and deserved individual attention. The older trees needed more experience to prune than the younger. It'd taken her years of watching her father prune before she had enough confidence to do it herself so to think of Levi out there with a saw hacking at her trees made her heart ache. When thoughts like that arose, she had to remind herself that they were no longer *her* trees and neither was the orchard hers.

She moved away from the window. She could no longer worry about the orchard she was no longer going to inherit. Being married to Carter and having their child was worth more than a hundred orchards. However, life would be wonderful if she could have it all.

In the back of her mind was the belief and faith that God always answered prayers even if He took longer than expected. And sometimes His answers came in unexpected ways. It wouldn't surprise her at all if one day the orchard landed back in her lap through some kind of miracle.

Be thankful for what you have, she cautioned herself.

Now that their baby had safely arrived into her world, it was time to think about her own orchard again. She'd left the planting up to her advisor, who was her late father's good friend. For some reason she hadn't seen him lately and she didn't know why. Surely they could start planting now. It was April, after all, the perfect time for planting.

With her baby now relaxed, finally resting her head against Florence's shoulder, she sat down on the couch and closed her eyes.

Sometimes she looked back fondly on her old life with Wilma and the girls and the way life used to be. It had been far more hectic and stressful, in those days, with the many roles she'd had to play—orchard manager, household manager, half-sister manager, and squabble manager. Then she had to wonder what her Amish bonnet sisters—as Carter called them— were doing today.

IN THE BAKERS' Apple Orchard household, Bliss Bruner sat at the kitchen table ready to pen a letter to Adam, her secret crush. Now that her stepsister Cherish no longer liked him, she hoped there might be a chance for her and she was ready to take a risk and find out.

She figured if she wrote thanking him for allowing her to have the rabbit, that would open up communication between them. He had been upset on hearing the rabbit had got away from their house where he was supposedly being kept safe, and had been chased by a dog. It made her like Adam more to know that he was so caring about animals.

"What are you doing?" Cherish breezed into the kitchen and sat down opposite, grabbing at her letter.

She batted Cherish's hand out of the way. "I'm writing a letter to Adam Wengerd."

Cherish leaned back into the chair. "Ah, that's a name I want to forget. For the past few days my anger has been brewing against him. It was a dreadful thing he did, telling me Bruiser was a male. Judging from all of his recent offspring, it's clear he's a she. The worst thing was, Adam made me a part of his deception because I then gave the rabbit to you and passed on the information he gave me."

"*Nee*, it was a mistake. No one would do that deliberately. You shouldn't let anger get a hold of you, Cherish."

"Don't you start. I'm tired of being told how I should

feel and how I should be all the time. *Don't be mad, forgive, let people trample all over you …"*

"You don't mind me writing to him, do you? I didn't think you still liked him. Do you?" Bliss held her breath. If Cherish said she did, then she wouldn't be able to write to him. It wouldn't be right. The only thing she could do was forget about him and look for someone else. Trouble was, there wasn't anyone as nice as he was.

Cherish made a sour face. "How could you think I still like him after everything that's gone on? Of course I don't. If he knocked on the door I wouldn't even talk to him. I'd close the door on him. Anyone would have to have lost their mind to like him." She tapped the side of her head.

"Well, I'll keep writing to him." Bliss looked down at the letter wishing Cherish would leave her in peace.

"Didn't you hear what I just said?" Cherish asked, leaning forward.

"I did and I respect your opinion about Adam but I don't share it."

Cherish's mouth dropped open. Normally, Bliss would've gone along with anything she said. "I'm angry at you for not being more sensitive to my feelings. You should be upset with Adam on my behalf since you keep going on about how pleased you are to have siblings at last and be part of such a large family. You should care more about me."

"Oh, Cherish, don't be mad. I just want to be happy and love everyone. I can't be happy when you're upset with me."

"Okay, well, I'm not upset with you. You can't help being weak-willed."

Bliss smiled. "Good. I'm not sure what you mean by that, but I'm pleased you're not angry with me."

Cherish's eyebrows drew together. "Adam was so awful to me and he didn't even wait to hear the full story."

"The full story about Cottonball?"

"Cottonball?"

Bliss's face lit up. *"Jah,* I've just decided to change his name ... her name, I mean, from Marshmallow to Cottonball."

Cherish rolled her eyes. "Just choose a name and stick with it, would you?"

"I have and ... I am. Cottonball. I thought of Snowball, but I know someone whose cat is named Snowball and I wanted something unique." Bliss looked back at the blank page and visions of Adam danced in front of her face. He was so handsome. "How shall I start the letter?"

"Dear Adam, I hope this letter finds you UNWELL."

"Unwell?" Bliss spluttered. "Cherish! How could you say that?"

CHAPTER 2

CHERISH GLARED AT HER STEPSISTER. "If we're ever to have a sister relationship, you'll have to understand me better. The thing is, I don't want to be nice. I've decided from now on I'll tell people exactly what I think of them. And I don't think very much of *him*. People have to learn when they've upset others, and how will he know if no one ever checks him?"

"It's not up to you."

"Jah it is. If he gets away with bad behavior he'll never know how awful he's been. Too many people in life don't go out of their way anymore to put things right. Everyone's leaving the hard stuff up to someone else. All I want to do is save the next person from getting deceived by Adam Wengerd." Cherish shuddered all over after she said his name.

"Why not just let it go? Forgive and forget. He's not even here anymore. He'll never bother you again."

"That is a very good point, Bliss, my dear chubby step-*schweschder*, but I have thought the whole thing through.

7

Just because I'm the youngest around here doesn't mean I'm not the smartest. As I've just been telling you, people shouldn't be allowed to get away with bad deeds."

"Do you want to be reminded of every error you've ever made?" Bliss asked. "I'm sure there are plenty of 'em."

Right now Cherish was wondering why *Mamm* couldn't have married someone other than Levi. Perhaps someone with younger children for her to boss about. Bliss was older so that meant another older sister—something she needed like their apple orchard needed Levi managing it. "What errors?"

"I can't recall them all because I don't keep track. I forgive people as I go along in life. I want to be happy. If I remembered every time someone wronged me I'd wear a permanent frown. Besides all that, you just called me *chubby*. That wasn't nice."

Cherish stood, leaned over and pinched Bliss's stomach through the folds of her dress.

"Ow!"

"I call it like I see it." She held her fingers up in the air, two inches apart. "That's how much you are chubby around the tummy, but don't worry. You might lose it when you get older and no one can see it under the big flappy dresses that you wear."

"I don't think I'm fat." Bliss looked down at her dresses. Was that the reason Adam never looked twice at her—she was fat and she wore flappy dresses? "Is something wrong with my dresses? I was thinking of sewing a new one."

"Who said fat? Besides, there's nothing wrong with

extra pounds, is there? It's good for horses and livestock. I mean, what do you think of an owner who has a horse with ribs sticking out? You think, *what a dreadful owner.* You're just well fed and that's a good thing. We're not starving you." Cherish grinned.

"So, I don't look bad the way I am?" Her greatest hope was that Adam would return to their community someday, but what was the point if he didn't like the way she looked when he got there?

"You look fine. You've got a pretty face."

Bliss smiled. *"Denke,* Cherish. When I see my reflection I honestly don't think I look too bad. I look okay."

"And when you're older, I'm sure all those freckles on your face will fade. And you'll need … you'll need some new dresses. You wear dresses that make you look twice your size. If you follow my advice, then a man might find you nice enough to marry one day."

That wiped the smile off Bliss's face. She wanted to be nice enough now. "Oh. I hope they do."

"Don't you have anything better to do than sit here and write a letter to someone you'll never see again, *schweschder* dear?"

Bliss smiled on hearing Cherish call her 'sister' rather than 'stepsister.' "That's right, so are you going to help me?"

Cherish pushed out her lips while she thought for a moment. "I'm having a rest before I pin the washing out. I don't mind helping you write the letter."

"Denke. Now how will I start?" Bliss sighed loudly and looked at the blank page once more. "I honestly have no idea and I've been thinking about it for a good half hour."

"I'll write it for you if you're so hopeless." She plucked the pen from Bliss's hand. Taking a firm grip, she wrote as she spoke. *"Dear Adam, I am writing to tell you that I'm very upset and disappointed in you."*

"Nee. That's not what I want to write. You sound like a cranky parent and not a friend." Bliss grabbed the paper from her and ripped it in two.

"Maybe his parents never told him not to be rude." Cherish said, "This is what you should write, listen up. *Dear Adam, I am writing to tell you that I'm very upset and disappointed in you. You were very rude to my stepsister, Cherish, when you heard that Bruiser got out and was chased by a dog. Both those things were outside of Cherish's control. You were so rude to her."*

Cherish looked up at Bliss when she breathed out a loud sigh. She couldn't tell Bliss that it was *Mamm* who had pushed the rabbit out the door and then laughed, saying they would tell Bliss that the rabbit escaped and ran away. Even Cherish had been shocked by her mother's cruelty and perhaps if she told Bliss what had happened she might not even believe her. Bliss thought the sun shone out of her stepmother and thought she could do no wrong. What she didn't know was that *Mamm* did a lot of things wrong. She didn't want to disappoint sweet and simple Bliss, so she kept quiet.

"Nee. Don't worry I'll write it myself." Bliss took a fresh piece of paper out of the box of stationery beside her. "Could you dry the dishes while I write?"

Cherish stood. "All right. And ask for my money back too while you're at it. It's not fair that he would charge me for something he misrepresented and that's what I truly believe." She leaned over the table and stared into Bliss's freckled face.

"Oh, that would be embarrassing. I want to write a friendly letter."

"That's okay. I don't need to ask for my money back. He's probably spent all of it by now anyway." She couldn't tell Bliss that she bought the rabbit for a dollar because she had flirted with him. Cherish wasn't happy with Bliss writing to Adam. She obviously liked him otherwise why even bother?

Just when Cherish was putting the last dish away, Bliss announced. "I'm finished. Do you want to read it?"

"Sure." Cherish wiped her hands and then sat opposite once more.

"I don't know what else to write. It is a very short letter."

Cherish read the boring letter full of nonsense and saying nothing. "Short and to the point. You've said what you had to say."

"Oh, I didn't write that Cottonwool had babies."

"Cottonwool?" Cherish's nose crinkled. Had Bliss changed the rabbit's name again? "You said his name was Cottonball."

"*Her* name, not *his* name. And you're right. It was Cottonwool, but it's Cottonball now." Bliss giggled. "I'll have to remember that myself."

"*Jah,* you should remember the name of your own rabbit." Cherish smiled, seeing the humor in the situation. Even though she'd found it a little bit funny when their 'male' rabbit had babies—and they were so cute—that in no way excused Adam for what he'd done. Despite what Adam thought, Cherish knew she was a good pet owner and was always kind to animals. She'd searched hours for the rabbit when her mother literally kicked the rabbit out of the house.

Cherish picked up the pen. "I'll add that for you at the bottom. Our writing is similar." Cherish spoke as she wrote. *"And we know she's a female now because she had babies. Four of them."*

"Good work," Bliss said. "That says it all. He'll make sure he does a better check of what he's selling in the future, now."

"Let's hope so." Cherish folded the letter into three. Looking up at her slightly older stepsister, she put her hand out. "Envelope?" Bliss looked in her box. When she saw there were no envelopes, she got up and ran to the next room, and came back with an envelope and gave it to Cherish. Without thanking her, Cherish pushed the letter into the envelope and licked it shut. Looking back at Bliss she said, "Stamp? It won't send without a stamp."

"I'll go look." Bliss got to her feet again and soon returned with a stamp. "Here you are."

"Denke, Bliss. How about we go into town and post it right now?"

"I'd love a trip to town. Can we stop somewhere and get a cappuccino?"

"Of course. I'll even buy it. My treat. We'll have to go to the café where I work though because I get a discount."

"Okay. Do you mind if I stop and ask for jobs along the way?"

"That'll be fine, I suppose. Yeah, why not?"

"Denke, Cherish. You're the best *schweschder* ever."

"I know, and it's step-*schweschder*. Since I'm treating you to coffee how about you do something for me?"

"*Jah*, anything."

"Pin the clothes out. I should've done that instead of what I did for you just now. It won't hurt you to do something for me."

"Sure. I'll do it now."

"Good. I'll go upstairs and change and then we can go. We'll have a lot of fun."

"*Wunderbaar*. I'll pin them out then meet you at the barn," Bliss said. *"Denke."*

As soon as Bliss was out the door, Cherish ripped open the envelope. Then she took a fresh sheet of paper and wrote what Bliss should've written if she was truly a loving and supportive stepsister.

CHAPTER 3

C HERISH HAD DECIDED Bliss's letter to Adam Wengerd was boring. She had ripped it up and she set about writing the letter she'd replace it with, posing as Bliss.

'Dear Adam, I need to tell you what I think of the way you treated my dear stepsister and sister in the Lord, Cherish. You sold her Bruiser as a boy when he was a girl. My guess is that you knew he was a girl and that girl bunnies would be harder to sell. You tricked her and I demand you give her a full written apology.'

She paused a moment. He was so handsome. Why did he have to turn out so horrible? It was a waste.

Continuing her letter, she wrote, *'Don't even bother writing one word back to me unless it starts with 'I'm sorry.' You were very unkind to Cherish and she is such a good and nice person she does not deserve your rudeness and neither does she deserve you judging her.'*

While Cherish was dreaming up some other nice things she could write about herself, she heard a horse and buggy arrive outside. Cherish quickly finished off the letter signing it 'Bliss.' She tore up the envelope she'd ripped open, along with Bliss's original letter, and threw them into the trash by the door.

Envelope! She needed a fresh one and she knew just where to get one and a stamp. Favor always had a good supply.

She burst into Favor's room to see her still in bed. "What are you doing, Sleepyhead? I thought you went with the rest of them."

"I don't feel well."

Cherish leaned forward and touched her forehead with the back of her hand. "You do feel hot. I'll get you a cool washcloth."

"*Denke.* And some water?"

"Sure. First, I need an envelope and a stamp. Bliss is sending a letter to that dreadful Adam Wengerd."

"Okay. At the bottom of my cupboard in a box."

Cherish flung open the cupboard door and found a stack of envelopes and at least a dozen stamps. "*Denke.* Bliss and I are heading into town. I guess you're too sick?"

"*Jah.*"

Cherish went downstairs, put the letter into the envelope and left it on the kitchen table. As she filled up a glass at the kitchen sink, she noticed it was Joy's buggy, but she couldn't see Joy anywhere; she wasn't tending to the horse that was just standing there still attached to the buggy. Cherish would find out what was going on. Meanwhile, she took the glass of water and a cool washcloth back upstairs. After she set the glass down on Favor's night-stand, she placed the cloth on her forehead. "How's that?"

"Good." Favor's eyes closed.

"Want me to bring you back something from town?"

"Nee denke. Close the curtains?"

"Sure." When she got to the window, she looked out to see Joy and Bliss talking. It looked like a serious conversation. She shut the curtains and went to see what was going on.

Before she got outside, she noticed the stamped envelope on the kitchen table. To get Adam's address, they'd have to stop at Mark's saddlery store. They'd have his address since he'd worked for them briefly while he was there.

As she pondered whether she'd be found out for posing as Bliss, she realized it was too late for regrets. She'd already ripped up Bliss's original letter.

"I'VE GOT SOME NEWS, BLISS."

Bliss dropped the dress back into the washing basket and hurried over to Joy who had just pulled up in the buggy. She always wanted to be the first to hear anything new and by the sounds of it Joy had some gossip. Normally, Joy wasn't the kind of person to spread rumors, so whatever news she had was sure to be true. "What is it?"

"I don't know why *Mamm* and Levi haven't told us yet, but I just met Ada on the way home. She was going one way in her buggy and I was going the other. We stopped on the road and talked." Joy took a deep breath.

Bliss knew something weird was going on. Joy looked so troubled. "Go on," Bliss urged.

"Did you know they're going away on a trip with *Mamm* and Levi?"

That was news to Bliss. No one had said a thing to her. "You mean like a vacation?"

"*Jah.*"

"*Nee.* I haven't heard that. Just by themselves … without us?"

"*Jah,* well we are all pretty much adults now so we can look after ourselves."

"You're married so I can understand why they wouldn't take you. We haven't been away as a family since *Dat* married Wilma. It would've been nice if we'd been included. That's what family's about, isn't it? I'm guessing they won't even ask us if we haven't been told by now. They just don't want us around."

"What do you care? You'll be here with Cherish, Favor and Hope without anyone watching over your shoulder."

Bliss knew that wasn't quite true. Joy would be there with Isaac, not too far from the *haus*. "When is it happening?"

"Week after next I think. She clammed up pretty quick when she realized I didn't know. It came up in conversation and if you ask me, Ada was quite surprised that I didn't know. Are you sure you didn't know? I would've thought your *vadder* might've mentioned it to you."

"Of course not, otherwise I would've said so just now."

Joy looked up at the sky. "My guess is they're going up

north to see Mercy and Honor's *bopplis* again. Ada would love to see them, I'm sure."

"We haven't even seen our own nephews. I guess they're my step-nephews, but I'll call them my nephews."

"*Jah* of course. They're your nephews. It's okay to say that."

"*Mamm* and *Dat* are selfish if they plan to go off by themselves. This is quite shocking behavior. I'm surprised at them." Bliss was never usually so outspoken, but she was upset. Before her father married Wilma, she'd had all of his attention. Now she had to share him with Wilma, with all her new step-siblings, and even with the apple orchard. It wasn't easy.

Joy suggested, "Why don't you ask your *vadder* about it?"

"*Nee*. I'll wait and see how long it takes them to tell us. Are you sure it's coming up so soon?"

"Ada didn't say too much. She clammed right up when she realized *Mamm* had not told us anything, but I'm guessing it's in the next week or two. Fairly soon. What are you doing today?"

"I've just got to pin the rest of these clothes out and then Cherish and I are going into town."

"Are you looking for work?"

"Favor's in bed not feeling well, and I'll look for work while we're there."

"That's too bad about Favor."

"She's starting to get those headaches *Mamm* gets."

Joy raised her eyebrows. "A 'for real headache' or a 'get out of work and spend the day in bed' type of headache?"

"I think she's really sick. Her cheeks are red and her face is hot. I'll check on her before we go."

"Ah, she can't fake that."

The two of them laughed.

"I should rub the horse down," Joy said. "Unless you want to take him into town? I haven't driven him far."

"Sure. Saves us some work. We'll be ready to go as soon as I do this."

"I'll help you." Joy walked over to the clothesline with Bliss.

CHAPTER 4

FLORENCE OPENED her front door with her crying baby in her arms. Carter had been to town and back to get the weekly food supplies, and Florence was completely exhausted because the baby had woken every hour for a feeding. Now she was allowing Carter to get some sleep and when he woke up, it would be her turn. "Christina, I'm so pleased to see you."

"Congratulations on your baby, Florence. I'm so happy for you both."

Florence knew that Christina had been aching to have a baby of her own for many years and it couldn't have brought her joy to see Florence holding a baby of her own so soon after being married. Christina and Mark had been childless for years. Christina leaned forward and kissed Florence on her cheek.

"Thank you, come in. Would you like to hold her?"

Christina's face lit up. "Would I ever."

Florence gladly passed the howling baby over to her friend and sister-in-law. Immediately, the baby stopped crying and closed her eyes and relaxed into Christina's shoulder. "Well, would you look at that? You've got the special touch with *bopplis.*"

"Do you think so?"

"Of course, look at her. She's been crying for so long, so unsettled and look at her now."

A smile beamed across Christina's face. "Mark is coming one day after work if that's suitable to you."

"Anytime suits us."

"He's so anxious to see his niece."

"Would you like a cup of hot tea?"

"No thank you. I'm just happy to sit down and cuddle this little one."

They sat down in the living room.

"Tell me what's going on with you, Christina? The girls told me that you and Mark went away and there are rumors you're looking for somewhere to move to? Tell me you're not moving away. I have so few friends and Earl's gone and not coming back. I don't want to lose Mark too."

Christina smiled. "I'm glad that you consider me a friend, Florence. We haven't always been close."

"Well, we are now. As close as we can be under the circumstances."

"That's true. We did go away. I just wanted a change. It seems every day is the same and I feel stuck. It's causing problems between Mark and myself. His store is doing well, bringing us in a good income and my sewing business is doing well, but I can move that anywhere. Anywhere, as long as the community is reasonably large and there are Mennonite communities nearby as well. Mark does not want to move, he told me. I don't know if I really do, but I just need something different. Now if I had a *boppli,* that would be enough to keep me happy and keep me busy."

"I'm sure you *will* have one soon."

"I don't think so. And I have to face that. With each passing year I'm getting older, my womb is drying up like a shriveled prune. The chance I had at being a mother is gone. I'm a sadness to myself and an even greater disappointment to Mark."

"Nee, don't say those things. Mark doesn't feel like that at all. He loves you."

She stared into Florence's eyes. "I don't know if he does. I think he reached a certain age and felt he should be married. I was just a convenience and now I'm a very large inconvenience, but he's stuck with me, so what can he do?"

"He loves you. And he loves you more and more with every passing year."

Christina sighed. "If only that were so. You and Carter are the real love match. There aren't many marriages around like yours."

Florence knew what she said was true. Many of the people in the community married someone thinking love would come later. Sometimes it did and sometimes it didn't, but by then there was nothing they could do. Divorce was not an option in the Amish community. If a couple couldn't live together they could choose to live separately, but so few chose that option. "I hear what you're saying. Carter and I do have a very special relationship, but so do you and Mark."

Christina gently jiggled the baby up and down on her

shoulder and patted her on the back. "If only that were true. If only … I can't help thinking he might love me more if I gave him a child."

"I think you're just looking for things to be worried and sad about."

"I don't think I am, Florence. I love him, but I feel he's just putting up with me. And don't you dare say anything to him about what we've said."

"Of course I won't. What is said between these four walls is just between you and me."

"Thank you, Florence." She looked at the baby. "She is falling asleep."

"Finally."

Christina reached down and kissed the baby on the forehead. "Hello, my young niece. I'm so happy to meet you."

"And she's very blessed to have her Auntie Christina."

"Thank you, Florence. I'll be the best aunty she ever had."

Florence giggled. "I don't doubt it for a moment, and you don't want to move away and miss her growing up, do you?"

"You're right. I must stay here and be in her life."

"Yes, that would make me and this little girl very happy."

"What's her name?" Christina asked. Florence opened her mouth, but Christina guessed what she was about to say. "Oh, Florence. Do you mean to tell me you don't have a name yet? You had all those months with her growing inside you and you couldn't come up with a name in all that time?"

"It's just that it's a very important thing and we don't want to name her after anyone we know, or the family knows. And every time I think of a name, I think of a person who has that name. We both just wanted her to have one that is uniquely her own name. Does that make sense?"

"Whatever her name is it will be uniquely her own."

"I don't mean it in that way."

"What about something to do with apples or the orchard?"

"Yes, we've been thinking along those lines, but nothing suits. We're running out of time. We have to submit the birth certificate soon. We've set a deadline for tonight because we're going to send the paperwork off tomorrow."

"Today is a very important day. Naming day."

"Yes, if we can't think of anything that we agree on we're just going to put names in a hat and pull one out."

"I hope you think of something very nice. I can give you some of my names that I've been thinking about. Rebecca, Rachel, Deanna, Mia, Adele, Adrina, Maddalena, Mary Lee, Eva, Ava ..."

"That's okay, we have a long list of possibilities."

"It would be a very hard decision to make, but it's a wonderful decision, too. She'll carry that name every day of her life."

"I know. Are you sure you don't want to have a cup of tea?"

"Okay, that sounds good as long as I don't have to put this little one down. Not until I'm drinking the tea of course. Wouldn't want to risk spilling it."

"Are you sure? She is quite heavy after a while."

"I'm sure." She rested her cheek on top of the baby's head.

"Come to the kitchen with me. We can talk more while the water boils."

CHAPTER 5

CHERISH AND BLISS had managed to get Adam's address from Mark at the saddlery store, and now Bliss stood in front of the mailbox while holding the letter addressed to Adam Wengerd.

"What are you waiting for?" Cherish yelled from the buggy. "We don't have all day. Just mail the thing already."

Bliss had second thoughts. Perhaps she'd rewrite it and say something better. The letter had been too hastily written. She headed back to the buggy with it clutched in her hand.

"What are you doing now?" Cherish asked when she got back into the buggy.

"I don't know. I'm nervous about what he'll think when he reads it. He'll know I like him and ... he might not be happy about it."

Cherish stared at the envelope. "We've gone to a lot of trouble to get his address and now you're not—"

"I know, Cherish, and I'm sorry. I can't help thinking

of that old saying, 'when in doubt don't.' And I have many doubts."

"You're just lacking in confidence. It's the right thing to do, trust me."

"Do you think so?"

"Jah. Give it to me. I'll do it."

Biting her lip, Bliss moved the letter closer to Cherish, who quickly plucked it from her fingers.

Cherish sighed as she jumped out of the buggy. "I have to do everything myself."

She held the letter over the opening of the letterbox and then allowed it to drop from her fingers. When she heard the gentle sound of it hitting the bottom, the real doubts started. Was the letter too harsh? No, she decided as she reminded herself of her earlier rant to Bliss. People like Adam should know the implications and outcome of their words and their actions. He looked down his nose at her and made her feel bad when nothing had been her fault at all. It irritated her every time she thought about it.

But what if Adam wrote back and Bliss found out she had substituted a not very nice letter of her own and sent it to him? What would Bliss do? Bliss said she forgives people, but would she forgive her for forgery? She even signed Bliss's own name.

There was only one answer to Cherish's problem.

She had to be the one—and the only one—who collected the mail for the next few weeks. If no letter came from Adam within that time frame, that meant he would never write back.

"Come on, Cherish, it can't take that long to post the letter." Bliss's giggles filled the air.

Cherish smiled. It seemed they both suffered from the same indecision when it came to Adam Wengerd, but for entirely different reasons.

"Come and take me up the road so I can stop in at a few places. You can write the name of the businesses down in the book."

Cherish looked up at her stepsister half hanging out of the buggy and whining at her. "Coming." Cherish got back into the buggy and Bliss handed her the book. Levi had ordered Favor and Bliss to write down all the places they inquired about possible employment every day. He threatened he would stop by these places and ask if they had indeed been there. Because it had taken them a long time looking, he didn't believe they were truly committed to finding work. That was partly true, but only because they had no real skills and they were so young. The jobs they could apply for were limited.

They could only work domestic duties such as cleaners or assistant cooks. All these jobs had many people applying for them. It wasn't helpful that they had no faster mode of transport than a horse and buggy. For every job, they were up against people who owned cars, or who lived closer, and they could be called into work at short notice. These were things Levi would not accept as excuses.

Levi was someone who only saw things in black-and-white.

"Cherish, before we go anywhere I have to tell you something."

Cherish didn't like the sound of that. "What is it?"

Bliss then told Cherish what Joy had told her about Levi and *Mamm* going away.

"Why didn't you tell me this before now—on the way into town?"

"I don't know. I just remembered it now. I thought you should know."

Cherish sighed. "I don't believe it. Joy must've heard wrong. *Mamm* would never go away without telling me. She'd go on her own like she did last time. I can understand her wanting a break from everyone. *Nee*, Joy has obviously misheard."

"Don't forget that things are different now for *Mamm*."

Cherish winced every time Bliss called her mother *Mamm*. She was her stepmother so she should've called her Wilma. "What things are different?"

"She has a new husband. Things are bound to change from how they've always been. Everyone's had adjustments to make. When *Mamm* went by herself last time, she and *Dat* were having problems. You know that. They're fine now. Whatever problems they've had have been worked out, so maybe they want time alone."

Cherish wouldn't hear of it and if she hadn't been holding the reins she would've blocked her ears. "She would've told me. I'm the youngest so she would've worried about me being okay and perhaps suggested I go along."

"Of course she's going to tell you and all of us, she just hasn't told us yet."

It unsettled Cherish that decisions like this could be made without her input. If her father were still alive he would've taken the whole family away, not just gone off alone with their mother. "What else did Joy say about it?"

"I don't have exact details. Joy wasn't sure. She thinks it's very soon, though. She said that Ada clammed up and acted surprised when she realized *Mamm* and *Dat* hadn't told us."

Cherish pressed her lips together, annoyed. "It's typical of *Mamm*, though, to only think of herself."

"Cherish, that's a terrible thing to say. Joy thinks *Mamm's* going to visit Mercy and Honor's babies again. It feels like she's only just come back, but it's been quite a few weeks—months even."

Now Cherish regretted saying anything at all. Why couldn't Bliss be more like Cherish's real sisters? She looked in the side mirror, pleased that the road wasn't busy today. She hated sharing the road with impatient cars. "I haven't even seen them yet. So unfair."

Bliss was concentrating on the line of stores they were passing. "Stop here. I'll ask at this mercantile place."

Cherish moved the buggy over and stopped behind a parked car. "Haven't you been there before? It looks familiar."

"A long time ago but it hasn't been written down in the book yet."

"Fine, off you go. I'll wait right here for you."

"*Denke.*"

Cherish sat there and watched her stepsister go into the mercantile building. It sold everything from fabrics to flashlights, metal pots to make up. It was a general store of sorts. She wasn't surprised to see Bliss come out only two minutes later. "Sorry that didn't work out for you."

31

Bliss sat down heavily and Cherish moved the horse and buggy forward. "They wrote my name down. And my phone number. They were surprised I had a phone connected. I told him that was the phone number in the barn. They looked at me like I was a little weird."

"Yeah, as if *that* hasn't happened before. All *Englischers* think we're weird."

"I know, I know they do. It doesn't bother me."

"Yeah, I guess I've gotten more used to it. Now where?"

"There's another store, stop here."

"Don't even bother," Cherish said when she saw Bliss staring at a boutique dress shop.

"I know they won't give me a job, but I do have to write something down for *Dat.*" Bliss handed her the book. "Write down this one and the mercantile."

"Okay." Cherish took the book from her and then Bliss got out of the buggy. It was all a ridiculous waste of time, but it proved that Bliss wasn't that different from her. It wasn't an entirely honest thing for Bliss to do, in Cherish's opinion. She was fooling her father by asking at places just so she'd have another name to write down in the book.

Once Cherish had made the notes in the book, she looked in the window and saw Bliss talking to a woman. Then the woman shook her head. Even though Bliss didn't expect to be given a job, that didn't stop her shoulders from drooping when she walked out.

"Another rejection," Bliss said when she climbed into the buggy next to her.

"Hey, don't get upset. You expected them to say no."

"I know that, but it still hurts." Bliss pouted making her cheeks more chubby.

"Working is not that great."

"It is. I would feel appreciated if someone paid me to do something. You get paid to make coffee and you must be so good at it because your customers even give you tips."

"Don't you dare tell your *vadder* about the tips."

"It's not my secret to tell, Cherish. That's up to you and your conscience and between you and *Gott.*"

"Yeah, I just don't want you opening your big mouth. I'll see what I can do to help you."

"What do you mean?"

"I could get one of the girls I'm working with fired and you could take her job."

Bliss's mouth fell open in shock. *"Nee,* don't do that!"

Cherish threw her head back and laughed. "Relax, it's just a joke. I'd never do anything like that. But seriously, I could ask the boss if you could maybe do a shift or two."

Bliss's mouth turned down at the corners. "I don't think *Dat* would like that. It seems he wants us to get full-time jobs or nothing."

"Jah, but what do *you* want? You're almost an adult now. And your *vadder* must think so too if he's willing to leave us all alone to go off around the countryside with *Mamm.*"

"You do have a good point."

"I know, don't I?"

Bliss fixed a smile on her face. "You do. Can you go there now and ask?"

"That's where we planned to go anyway, remember?"

"Ach, jah." Bliss giggled. "I'd forgotten already."

"Just as well one of us has her thinking cap on. We're going there right now and I'm going to get us coffee and cake or pie, and I'll ask my boss, if he's there."

"Thank you, Cherish. You're the best *schweschder* ever." She put her head on Cherish's shoulder.

Cherish cleared her throat. "Step-*schweschder*, remember that."

"Jah, I know. It's all the same to me. We're family now, Cherish, don't you think so?"

"Hmm, I guess we are." Cherish gave Bliss a big smile. She meant well even if she was a little annoying at times.

CHAPTER 6

BACK AT HOME when Favor heard the girls leave, she got out of bed to get her writing implements, then got back in bed and started writing a letter of her own. She wanted a day home alone by herself with peace and quiet. *Mamm* and Levi had gone somewhere together, Hope was at work, and she knew Cherish and Bliss wouldn't be in any hurry to come home and do chores.

Her plan had worked. She wasn't lying about having a headache. She had one, but it wasn't bad enough to cause her to stay in bed all day.

She wrote to Caroline. What she really wanted to do was invite Caroline to stay. They'd talked about it many times through their letters—where they'd go and what they'd do. For now though, she'd have to write a normal letter rather than the one she wanted to write, actually inviting her to stay. Recently Levi had said she could have one of her pen pals stay, he just hadn't committed to the timeframe. Right now, that was as good as him saying no.

~

WHEN CHERISH and Bliss walked into the café where Cherish worked, Cherish whispered to Bliss, "We've got a new owner. The place is under new management."

"You didn't tell me that."

"That's because it's got nothing to do with you."

"I thought you would've said something."

"There was no need. Anyway, the manager … his name is Rocky. He really likes me. He thinks I'm doing a great job, so he'll listen when I recommend you."

"Why isn't he giving you more hours, then?"

"Because I don't want any."

"But *Dat* wants you to work more."

"What he wants and what I want are two different things."

"Oh, Cherish, isn't it being dishonest again? We have to be obedient to our parents."

"Well, considering at my age I'm almost an adult, and he's not my real parent, I think I can cancel out being pushed around by him and what he dictates." Cherish gave Bliss a nudge directing her to a table at the back. As soon as they sat down, Cherish nodded her head towards the counter. "That's Rocky, the one in the red T-shirt." He was a middle-aged man with a slightly receding hairline. Today he wore his T-shirt with the sleeves rolled up to reveal tanned well-muscled arms.

"He's your boss?"

"*Jah.* What do you want? I'll get you a cappuccino and a piece of pie."

"That would be fine *denke*, Cherish."

"You're welcome." She went to the counter and Rocky came forward to greet her. "That's my stepsister, Bliss over there. She desperately needs a job and she's such a hard worker, maybe even better than I am. Can you give her some work even for just an hour or two every week?"

"I'll have to give her four hours at the very minimum. Has she done this kind of work before?"

"No, but she's a fast learner. She just needs a start somewhere. She's very honest, reliable, and ... and all that."

"I could give her four hours every Wednesday or Tuesday morning. It depends on the week. Jasmine's just told me she's doing some kind of course and she'll be away at those times."

"For real?" Cherish hadn't expected that answer.

He smiled and nodded. "Yeah."

"Do you want to talk with her? That's her sitting over there."

"Sure."

Cherish waved her over and Bliss hurried over.

"Hi, I'm Bliss."

He put out his hand and she shook it. "Pleased to meet you, Bliss. I hear you're looking for work?"

"I sure am. I'll do any kind of work you've got."

He smiled. "I do have an opening on the roster for a few hours a week on either a Tuesday or a Wednesday morning."

"You do?"

"Yes. For someone who can make coffees." He tapped the large coffee machine to his left. "On this."

The smile left her face. "I haven't made coffee from a machine like that, but I'm sure I could learn."

"We'll train you."

"It's easy, Bliss. She'll do it," Cherish told him.

"Yes, I can do it." Bliss nodded enthusiastically.

"I like your energy, Bliss." He chuckled. "Are you good with numbers, money?"

"Very good."

"The till works out most of it. You just have to count out the right change."

"That's easy. I'm good at giving change. You can test me if you want."

"I'll take your word for it," Rocky said.

"Bliss has worked on lots of stalls and handled the money."

"Good. Good to hear. Well, you've officially got yourself a job Bliss Baker."

That last comment raised Cherish's hackles. While Bliss was nearly jumping up and down with excitement at just getting her first real job, Cherish had to correct him. "Oh, no she's not a Baker. She's my stepsister. She's a Bruner."

"My apologies. I'll see you bright and early next Tuesday, Bliss Bruner. You have the same phone numbers as one another?"

"Yes we live in the same house and you can reach us from the phone in the barn, and that's the number you have," Cherish said.

"Thanks so much, Rocky. I'm so grateful and I'll do an excellent job for you. I'll never let you down."

He chuckled. "Somehow, I believe you. Now can I get

you girls something to eat or did you just come here to see about a job?"

"We'll have two pieces of peach pie and two cappuccinos, please," Cherish said.

"Coming right up."

"Thanks."

"Don't we have to pay for that?" Bliss asked on the way back to the table.

"We can either pay at the end or at the start. I'll pay before we leave."

"Gotcha. Good to know."

"Yes, don't worry. Everything is easy to pick up. You'll be an expert in no time."

"Thanks so much, Cherish. I'm so pleased to get a job. Now I just have to make *Dat* see that part-time work is better than no work." The girls sat back down at the table.

"Exactly, and you'll be getting experience which will help you get a job somewhere else if you decide to do that."

"That's true. I feel like a real adult. I've got a part-time job. I can't wait to get my first pay. My money and mine alone. Oh, except that I have to give it over to *Dat*."

"Jah, but don't worry, you'll get tips. You have to be nice to people and get to know everyone's names. Most of the regulars are pretty good tippers. Especially the businessmen and the tradesmen who come for take-out." She gave Bliss a wink and Bliss giggled.

"I don't know if I'll be as good at that sort of thing as you."

"Of course you won't, but the closer you get to being as good as me, the more money you'll make."

"I'll remember that. I want to work until I get married then all I want to do is stay at home and have my man look after me." Bliss sighed with a dreamy look in her eyes. "I want to stay home all day being a *mudder*. What about you?"

"I've got the farm, silly. I know what's going to happen. I'm going to move to the farm as soon as I'm old enough and then my real life will start."

"This is your real life."

Cherish shook her head. "This life I'm living now is doing what everyone else wants." It was hard being the youngest.

"*Jah,* but isn't that kind of nice? I feel protected having *Mamm* and *Dat* make decisions for us."

"Each to their own."

Bliss giggled. "We're so different. That's why I like being in this family. Everyone is so different. It's never boring."

Cherish nodded. She could see the life Bliss had before would've been insufferably boring, living in a house with just Levi. *Poor Bliss.*

Several minutes later, Brooke brought over their pies and cappuccinos. Cherish introduced the two of them. When Brooke left, Bliss said, "I should've watched how they make the coffees."

"No need. Today we are the customers."

"Okay. Customers."

"That's right we are customers and…"

"Does that mean we have to leave them a tip?"

"*Jah,* I guess so, but not too much. We don't divide tips you know. Each person gets to keep their own."

"Okay. I've got a lot to learn and to remember."

"Just do an excellent job or it'll reflect badly on me."

"I will. Do you think we'll be working together?" Bliss took a sip of coffee.

"*Nee.*" Cherish looked down at the coffee and carefully folded the chocolate sprinkles into the milk froth with a spoon.

"It might be difficult for me to get here."

"This is no time to be thinking about that. You should've thought of that before you said yes to the job."

"It shouldn't be a problem. You always manage to get here. I just always think of the good and the bad side of things."

"Well that sounds like a complete waste of time. Just think about the good bits." Cherish picked up her coffee cup with both hands and took a sip, careful not to leave a froth mustache on her upper lip.

"Yeah, but you know what the job is like."

"I do. Just get your story ready for Levi. We'll have to convince him that this job will be good for you."

"I wish I didn't have to." Bliss pushed her fork into the pie, broke off a piece and popped it into her mouth. "Mmm, this is so good."

"You'll have to taste everything on the menu so you know what to recommend to people if they ask for suggestions."

"Okay. I will. *Denke* for doing this for me, Cherish. You're the best sis—um, step-*schweschder* ever."

"I think so; it's true."

The girls leaned in and giggled. Bliss wasn't so bad. She felt sorry for her that her mother had died. No wonder Bliss was so happy to have a family with the girls to keep her company. Then and there, Cherish decided to make a real effort to be nicer to her.

Cherish suggested, "Why don't we fill in time until we have to collect Hope from the B&B? There's no point in going home and then going back out again."

"That sounds good to me. All that's waiting for us at home is chores and we can do them when we get back if we do them really fast. What if we leave some of them for tomorrow?"

Cherish smiled at Bliss. They weren't that different deep down.

CHAPTER 7

FLORENCE WOKE from her second nap of the day to see that she was in her bedroom. She was certain she'd fallen asleep on the couch, but maybe that was this morning. Or was it yesterday?

When she opened her eyes fully, she was surprised to see Carter standing near her bed smiling. Normally, one or the other of them held the baby because she cried so much if she wasn't held. It was probably a bad parenting habit, but they all needed sleep and Florence couldn't bring herself to leave her baby in the crib and just let her cry.

"Where's the baby?" she asked, seeing Carter didn't have her in his arms.

"She's asleep in the crib, finally. I put her down when she fell asleep and she opened her eyes and then went back to sleep."

She stared at him for a moment. He had a secretive smile. "What's going on?"

"I have a surprise for you."

43

She sat up straight. "For me?"

"Yes. Unless there's another Florence hiding around here somewhere." He looked about.

"No, only the one."

"Come downstairs."

They walked down the stairs together and then Carter grabbed her hand and took her to the door. When he opened it, she saw two trucks and five men unloading plants. Then she saw Eric Brosley.

"Carter, is this ... is this what I think?"

"Yes, they're about to plant."

Florence's other hand flew to her mouth as she felt tears stinging behind her eyes. This was really happening. Eric looked over at them, and then walked toward them with a big smile. "I hear congratulations are in order."

"Yes, thank you."

"Carter told me you had a girl."

"Yes, we did. And ... I had no idea we were ready to plant. I've had my mind on other things."

"Carter and I have kept in touch. We didn't want to bother you with details under the circumstances."

She looked up at Carter wanting to tell him she'd been on bed rest not mind rest.

"I wanted to surprise you," he said.

She put both arms around Carter. "Thank you. This is the best surprise ever."

"Well, we'll get started. The men are fully trained and know what to do. Don't worry."

Florence smiled at Eric. "I'm not worried. I trust you completely."

"I'll make this orchard as good as I can." Eric took a

quick look behind him at the orchard next door. "We might try and make it better than that one." He threw his head to the side. Gave them a grin and headed back to the trucks.

"Thank you, Carter."

"This is our dream. Our plan is unfolding."

"It is, before our eyes. I have to take pictures of this."

Carter pulled his phone out of his pocket. "I'll take photos. That way we'll remember everything. You go inside and rest. I'll take some snaps and be in soon."

Florence walked inside and looked out the window. Her life was taking shape. God had blessed her with Carter, they had a baby, and now her orchard was taking shape. It would be years until those trees bore fruit, but that didn't matter.

Her thoughts returned to the day Carter asked her to run away and marry him. It had been a huge decision, but not a hard one. Back then she didn't know what the rest of her life would look like, but now she knew she and Carter were creating it themselves. Each decision they made was a tiny brushstroke forming the picture of their life. She was loving how the picture was forming.

CHAPTER 8

CHERISH AND BLISS pulled up outside the B&B at two in the afternoon. Hope climbed into the back of the buggy. *"Denke* for collecting me. I just couldn't face the ride home again. It's tough riding the bike here and back six days a week."

"I got a job," said Bliss with a huge grin as she turned around from the front seat to face Hope.

"You did?"

Bliss and Cherish had changed positions. Now Bliss was doing the driving. She jangled the reins and the horse moved on.

"Jah, she got a job where I work. It's just a four-hour shift and she starts on Tuesday, the week after next."

"Why couldn't they have just given you the hours, Cherish?" asked Hope.

Cherish bit her lip. "You don't think Levi will think of that, do you?"

"I think that's the very first thing he'll think of. He's always telling you to get more hours. Now you've both

47

got a few hours and you know he won't like it. I'm sorry, Bliss, I know you're excited and everything but I'm just thinking of what your *vadder* will say."

Cherish said, "I'm happy with what I'm doing. If I did any more I'd hate going to work. I'm just young and want to enjoy myself. Besides, I'm set up for my future because of dear Dagmar. I don't have to worry about a thing."

Bliss said, "I know what you're saying Hope and it's true. I figure if I start work with this job, then after a while I'll have experience and someone else might hire me full time."

"That's true. It won't be long before you have café experience. But, Cherish, you know Levi wanted you to get more hours."

"I know but it was either me or Bliss and now as Bliss just said, she gets the experience."

"And that's just how you should put it to Levi," Hope said.

Cherish and Bliss exchanged smiles. "*Denke*, Hope," they said as one.

"Do you think we could go past the Millers' farm?"

"Sure, if you want," Bliss said. "Are you going to stop in and see Fairfax?"

"*Nee*. He'd be working. I don't want to disturb him and besides those considerations, we can't really be seen to be too friendly. Not until he's had the instructions and gets baptized."

"You haven't been baptized yet, Hope, have you?" Bliss asked.

"*Nee*. We'll do it around the same time."

"Why do you want to drive past, then?" said Cherish craning her neck behind her to look at Hope.

"Because I miss him. I haven't seen him for a few days, but it feels like forever."

Instead of going straight ahead for home, they took a left turn.

"Don't go too slow when we get there. I don't want to look too obvious, like we're trying to see him."

"I hope they don't catch sight of us," said Bliss, "because this road doesn't really go anywhere."

"Go slow when we get there and I'll lower myself so no one sees me."

When they drove past the dairy farm, Hope saw Fairfax in the distance. "There he is. I don't know what he's doing."

Cherish caught sight of him. "He's looking around this way and that like he's lost."

"Maybe that's how he feels," said Bliss. "Lost?"

"Ach nee. Do you think that's how he feels?"

Cherish nudged Bliss. "I certainly don't think that. He's just having a quiet moment to himself. He works so hard, he's entitled to a moment."

"Dairy farms are hard work," said Bliss. "I didn't mean what I said before, Hope. Should we stop? He might see us and come over and then you'll get to talk to him. People will see and think we're just neighbors talking."

"Nee, just keep going home—the back-way home."

"Sure, if that's what you want," said Bliss.

The rest of the way home Hope worried about Fairfax feeling lost. Was that how he felt?

As soon as they got home, Cherish jumped out of the

buggy. "I'm going to check on Favor. Hope, you won't mind helping Bliss unhitch the buggy will you since we collected you and saved you riding your bike?"

"I don't mind at all. It's a good exchange."

Bliss pouted. "Why don't you help and I'll check on Favor?"

"Because I just got you a job today, so that's the very least you could do, don't you think?"

Bliss grinned. "Sure. And thanks again, Cherish."

Cherish walked to the house. There was nothing she liked better than getting out of work. Her dog, Caramel and Joy's dog, Goldie, ran to her. She crouched down to pet both of them. "I hope you've both been good today."

When she spied her mother bringing in the washing, she knew she was going to get a lecture. They should've been home a long time ago. *Mamm* would complain that she'd been left the chores to do on her own.

Cherish left the dogs and while her mother was out behind the house, she ran through the front doorway and scrambled up the stairs to see Favor.

When she reached Favor's bedroom she was surprised to see the door shut. She listened and when she didn't hear anything, she pushed the door open.

Favor was sitting up in bed, propped up with pillows, as though there was nothing wrong with her. Not only that, she was writing a letter. When Cherish looked harder, she saw Favor was surrounded by letters. They were strewn all over her bed.

"What is the meaning of this? Don't you have a headache?" Cherish sat down on the side of her bed.

"I do have a headache, but it's a little better now. Enough for me to write letters."

"That sounds a bit suspicious." Cherish grabbed the letter in her hands and stood up to read it.

"Give that back " Favor leaped up and managed to snatch it back and then settled back down on the bed. "You've got no right to read my mail."

"Well technically it's not your mail. It's just a letter you're halfway through writing. And Caroline ... isn't she an *Englisher?*"

"I'm allowed to have *English* pen pals."

"*Jah,* but you're not allowed to invite them to stay."

"Oh, you saw that?"

"I'm a fast reader."

"You heard Levi say that I could have a pen pal come to stay "

"He didn't say when and he didn't say you could have an *Englisher* come here and stay in this *haus.* It's just some-thing he says to keep you happy and stop you nagging. *Mamm* does the same thing. She tells you what you want to hear, but she never intends to give you what you want. And they call me deceptive." Cherish shook her head.

Bliss appeared in the room. "What's going on?"

Cherish sat back on the bed. "She's invited an *Englisher* to stay here without asking for permission. Did you leave Hope to rub the horse down and unhitch—"

"She said it was okay. Did you really do that, Favor?"

"*Jah,* I did. I'm writing the letter now. Levi said someone could come to stay and I'm holding onto that. He wouldn't have said it if he didn't mean it."

"Wow, you're going to get into the biggest trouble. I

heard what he said and he didn't say anything about an *Englisher*."

Cherish smiled. "That's what I said."

Bliss sat on the other side of Favor's bed.

"I don't see why."

"As soon as Levi and *Mamm* find out she's an *Englisher* they're not going to allow it."

Favor looked down at her letter. "She's a good girl and very quiet. It'll be fine. I know her really well. I've been writing to her since we've both been about ten years old."

"Still, you'll get into trouble."

"She might not even be allowed to come here to stay. She lives in California and it's such a long distance to come here."

"Why did you choose her? Why not someone from a different community?"

"Because she's the one I've always wanted to meet. We've always promised each other we will meet one day, no matter what. And I've been asking and asking for years. You know I have, Cherish."

"Yeah, asking and asking and being told no. I can't think *Mamm* would've been too happy with Levi allowing it."

"I'm just holding them to their word."

Bliss sighed. "So what's going to happen?"

"I'm going to send this letter and then wait for a reply. That's what's going to happen."

"We'll pray for you then, Favor. For lying about being sick and forgetting the problem," Bliss said.

Both sisters stared at her. "What problem?" Favor asked.

"The problem you were supposed to be sick with."

"I had a headache this morning and it's gone. One thing I know for sure is that *Mamm's* angry with both of you for being out all day."

"Cherish—the washing! We'll have to get it off the line." Bliss jumped up.

"Too late. I saw *Mamm* doing that when we got home."

"You're both going to be in big trouble." Favor smirked.

"It'll be okay when *Mamm* finds out that we took so long because Bliss has gotten herself a job."

That wiped the smile off Favor's face. "She did?"

"*Jah*, I did."

Favor groaned. "Now there's going to be even more pressure on me."

When Cherish saw Bliss open her mouth to tell her it was only for a few hours a week, she thought Favor should suffer a bit before she found out the details. "Let's go, Bliss. We'll have to tell *Mamm* the good news."

"Oh, *jah*. *Mamm* will be so pleased."

The girls left Favor alone with her letters.

CHAPTER 9

CARTER PICKED up a list of names and looked at Florence who was on the couch cradling their baby in her arms. Spot was snuggled next to her. Spot was fascinated by the baby and always stayed close. Carter sat down on the couch with Spot between Florence and himself. "Well, we said tonight's the night. We've run out of time."

"I didn't know it would be this hard," said Florence.

"I know, but none of the names we've thought of feels like a good fit to me. I've had some extra thoughts, though."

Florence was glad to hear it. "Me too, but tell me yours first."

"No you tell me yours first."

Florence laughed. "Okay. I know we said we wouldn't name her after anybody, but there is someone special from your life that I think we should consider."

His eyes sparkled. "Iris?"

"Yes. Your adopted mother and Wilma's sister."

"And my aunt, which is kind of weird."

"What do you think if we call our little girl Iris?" Florence held her breath hoping he'd approve. If not, their child might grow up to be the first nameless person on the planet.

"Most definitely. That's what I was thinking, too, but I didn't know what you'd think about it."

Florence heaved a sigh. "Perfect. We agree."

"What was your mother's name?"

While she thought about her mother and missed her every day, she didn't think of her as Eleanor, and strangely enough she didn't think of her as *Mamm* either. The only person she remembered calling *Mamm* was Wilma. "Eleanor," she said softly as her gaze traveled to the mantle, to the photo of Eleanor as a young woman before she joined the community to marry her father.

"That's right. I should've remembered," Carter said. "Iris Eleanor Braithwaite. What do you think?"

"I love it. It feels like a perfect fit. And it honors the women who are so dear to us."

"We finally have a name." He leaned forward and picked up the papers and Florence looked on as he carefully filled them in, asking her help to be sure he spelled 'Eleanor' correctly. "I'll go to town to post this first thing tomorrow."

"Okay. I'm glad that decision is over. It was a hard one to make."

"Yes it was. Next time we should think about names for boys and girls ahead of time so we're more prepared."

Florence smiled at the thought of having more children. They'd always planned to have a few and each baby that came would add more happiness to their lives. Hopefully Iris would be a good sleeper before the next one came along.

On Saturday afternoon, Cherish had sneaked upstairs to have a lie-down. Levi had everyone cleaning the outside of the house and Cherish and Bliss had been given the job of making sure the windows were spotless. It was a silly day to wash the house because it was windy. Levi thought it was a good day because it would dry faster. He didn't realize along with the wind came the dust. The season had been a dry one and dust from fields near and far had decided to land on their house. It wasn't any use telling Levi, though, because he rarely listened to anyone.

Just as she was drifting off to sleep her mother burst through her bedroom door.

"There's someone at the door to see you, Cherish."

She sat bolt upright. "I was only lying down for a moment. Who is it?"

"It's Adam Wengerd"

Cherish held her stomach. "Adam Wengerd is here?"

"Jah, jah."

Cherish scratched the back of her neck and then adjusted her prayer *kapp*. "And … he wants to see me?"

"He asked for you. Hurry, you can't keep him waiting."

Her blood ran cold. Had he discovered her deception? Did Bliss already know she'd written that letter pretending to be her?

This was the worst thing she'd done for some time, and now it had come full circle.

CHAPTER 10

As Cherish followed her mother down the stairs, all the reasons Adam Wengerd might've come to her house to ask for her ran through her head. Was he there to show her mother the letter she wrote to him? She'd never hear the end of it if her mother knew what she'd said. She'd tear strips off her for being so rude. When she got downstairs, Adam filled the doorway as he stood with his hat in his hands and his golden-toned hair smoothed back. "Adam, what a ... lovely surprise."

"Can I come in?"

"Of course." She looked around to see where her mother was. She'd disappeared and then she heard her sisters giggling in the kitchen. "Let's sit here on the couch. Can I get you something, cider, tea, coffee? You said, 'water.' Is that all, a glass of water?"

"I haven't said anything. I can't get a word in."

Once he sat, she asked, "Cookies, cake?"

He shook his head and then placed his hat on his knees. Politeness dictated she should've already offered to take his hat from him, but she had bigger problems than that.

From the expression on his face he didn't seem like he'd come there to get her into trouble. Now she had to add an apology to her ramblings. She wouldn't have written that letter if she thought there was even the slightest chance she'd ever have to see him again.

"I've got nothing left to offer you unless you'd like to stay for lunch. I believe we're having pork and cabbage rolls."

"That sounds delightful, but I'm here about a letter Bliss wrote me."

He knew!

She placed both hands in her lap and looked down. "I'm sorry about that. I have a great temper sometimes and I regretted it as soon as I sent the stupid thing, but by then it was too late. I couldn't reach into the postal box and get the letter back out."

He chuckled. "I'm not sure what you mean, but I'm here to apologize to you."

Was he trying to fool her? "You've come to apologize to me?"

He smiled. "That's what I just said. Although, I'm willing to accept your apology about whatever it was since you offered it. You said something about sending me that letter?"

"Oh, I posted the letter was what I meant." She'd been caught in a lie and as she was finding out, one lie always needed company. "You see, Bliss wrote it and I offered to post it, but then I was tardy. I should've posted it sooner."

"I see. No problem."

"Well, I was justified in being upset with you, don't you think?"

"Exactly. What part of what I did upset you the most?" he asked, almost smiling.

By now Cherish's head was spinning and since he was there to apologize, she was back to liking him again. "What did you do again?"

"I said some horrible things to you when I heard Bruiser got out. I know it wasn't your fault. I let anger get the better of me. Everyone says that you're a good and caring pet owner."

"It's true I am, and him ... her getting out was not my fault. Not my fault at all, so you're right about that."

"Bliss said in her letter that the rabbit had babies?"

"Yes. Four balls of fluff. They're delightful."

"What does Bliss plan to do with them?"

"Well, my *mudder* won't let us keep them all. I would very much like to. I suppose we'll have to find owners. It's really up to Bliss because they're her rabbits now."

"Where is Bliss? I'd love to see her. I thought she was a quiet girl, but now I know she's feisty."

His grin told her he liked the girl who wrote the letter. Now she couldn't tell him it was her. She was the one he really liked because she wrote the letter. "Bliss goes out most days looking for a job." It wasn't a lie, it was the truth. Bliss just happened to be home on this particular day. Cherish just hoped she wouldn't walk out of the kitchen any minute.

He stood. "I'm going to be staying here for a couple of weeks. Or maybe more, so I'll see more of you and your sisters."

That was good news to Cherish's ears. "Yes if you're staying here I suppose we will see you."

He flashed her a smile and her heart gave a flutter. Sure he had a hot temper and had said some horrible things, but so had she. She couldn't hold that against him. She walked him to the door. "Who are you staying with, Adam?"

He turned around and looked at her. "I'm staying with the Millers."

"Which Millers? There are several Miller households in this community. Not several, exactly, but a few."

"The Millers at the end of Pebble Creek Road."

"Fairfax is staying with them too and working on their dairy farm."

"Yes, I know. We're sharing the *grossdawdi haus* while I'm there. He talks about you and your sisters a lot."

"When did you arrive?"

"Yesterday morning."

"Thanks for stopping by."

"Nice to see you again, Cherish."

She smiled at him and gave a little wave. Then she stood on the porch watching while he got into the buggy and drove away.

Bliss joined her on the porch. "Did he ask about me?"

"He came to say he was sorry for the horrible things he said about me not being rabbit-worthy."

"Rabbit what?"

"Not worthy of owning a rabbit."

"Is that when Snowball was chased by Spot?" asked Favor.

Cherish turned around to see Favor, who'd just walked out of the house. "I believe it's Cottonball now, and yes."

In an exaggerated manner, Favor threw her hands in the air. "I can't keep up."

Cherish continued, "Cottonball got out and he blamed me, but now he knows it wasn't my fault so he came to apologize because he was mean and horrid."

Bliss smiled. "That's good that he apologized. That means he's a good and humble person."

"Do you still like him, Cherish?" Favor asked. "I know you did and then you didn't, but he has apologized and surely that must make you have second thoughts about ruling him out."

Cherish didn't want to admit to anyone that she liked him. "He's alright."

They might do something obvious to push the two of them together and that might drive him away. She figured the subtle approach was best. There was nothing subtle about her sisters at all.

"We'll see him at the meeting if he's staying at the dairy farm."

Cherish gasped and stared at Bliss. "You heard?"

"I heard most of what you and he said. Not all of it. I wished he would've come to see me. Maybe he didn't get my letter before he left."

Cherish hoped she hadn't said anything mean about Bliss. She couldn't remember. It was bad enough she made him think she wasn't there. Now Adam liked Bliss, and she had to do something to make him like her again.

CHAPTER 11

HOPE HAD WAITED and waited for the Sunday meeting to come so she could see Fairfax. With one of her sisters on each side, she walked into the Hershbergers' house where the meeting was being hosted. They sat on the very last bench at the back of the room. They always chose to sit at the back where they had the best view of who was coming and going.

She held her breath when Fairfax walked into the room. He looked handsome in his billowing white shirt, black suspenders and black pants. In those clothes, he seemed the same as every other Amish man, only more handsome.

Fairfax, along with Adam Wengerd, sat on the opposite side of the room. Like at all meetings, the men sat on one side and the women on the other.

Adam turned around and smiled at one of her sisters, she didn't know which one. Then Fairfax turned and when their eyes met, he smiled. She couldn't wait to find a private moment after the meeting to speak with him.

Throughout the meeting, Hope did her best to concentrate but that was hard because her eyes were fixed on the back of Fairfax's head. She wanted him to be absorbing every word of what the bishop said. The quicker he learned, the better he'd understand the world he was becoming a part of.

Their chance to talk came when everyone was busy with the meal afterward. The food was served in bowls in the middle of the long tables. Everyone would take a plate and help themselves.

When Hope sat down with her sisters after filling her plate, Fairfax walked over. Hope stood up and moved away from the table to talk to him.

"Hi, should we be speaking?"

"We aren't doing anything wrong, we're just talking."

"That's true. Can we speak in private?"

"Wait five minutes. Most everyone should be sitting down by then. Meet me behind the barn." She nodded towards the red barn around thirty yards away.

"Sure."

"Make sure no one sees you."

"I will."

Hope ate in a hurry and when she saw Fairfax head to the barn, she left the table and walked over around the other side of the barn to meet him. When they saw each other they ran towards each other and embraced.

"I miss you so much, Hope."

"Me too. It's quite impossible not seeing you every day like we used to."

"It won't be that long and we can be together all day every day. Apart from when I'm working."

"Tell me, how are you doing?"

"I'm fine." He held her at arm's length smiling and then pulled her back into his arms. "What about you?"

She didn't answer his question. "I saw you in the paddock and you looked a little bit unsure or uncertain."

"When did you see me?"

"Friday afternoon. I went past in the buggy."

"It's nothing. I'm handling everything well. It's not as hard as I thought."

She could tell from his face he wasn't being totally honest. "I'm guessing this will be the hardest thing you have to do. Then we'll be together."

His face relaxed into a smile. "I know. It'll be worth it at the end of the day when I get through everything and then we get married."

"I can't wait."

"Can you meet me tomorrow afternoon outside Carter and Florence's place? I want to thank them for all they've done for me."

"Sure. I'll take any excuse to see my niece again."

"I didn't properly explain why I left working for them. I'm sure they wanted me to work the place when my folks leave."

"Maybe we could do that. Could we run the orchard when your folks move?"

"Hey, I hadn't thought of that. It all seems such a long way off. I don't want to make promises that I won't be able to keep. I can't mention that to them."

Hope smiled. "I know. I'm always getting ahead of myself."

"Meet me at four tomorrow at their front gate?"

"I'll be there."

The two of them hugged again.

"What is the meaning of this? Are you lost, Fairfax?"

They sprang apart at the sound of the booming voice. It was Mr. Hershberger, one of the elders and the owner of the house where the meeting was being held.

"No, I'm sorry. I just wanted a quiet moment with Hope."

He stared at Hope, who didn't know what to say, and then he looked back at Fairfax. "This is not a good start for you. I think for both your sakes you better rethink decisions like this in the future."

Hope held her breath hoping he wasn't going to tell the bishop.

"Finish your meals and then I think you should both go home and not stay for the singing."

Hope was relieved. They were getting off lightly.

"I'm sorry, Mr. Hershberger," Hope said.

"I'm sorry too," said Fairfax.

The two of them walked back to the outside eating area with Mr. Hershberger following them.

She sat down with Cherish in front of her empty plate.

"What happened with Fairfax?" Cherish asked.

"Nothing much, we hugged."

"Why do you look so upset?"

"Mr. Hershberger saw us," Hope whispered.

"*Nee.*"

"It's okay. I don't think he'll say anything."

"You'll have to be more careful in future, Hope," whispered Favor.

"There is no future. I can't be alone with him now

until he's finished his time with the Millers. That's alright. I'll still be able to see him at the meetings and all our get-togethers. I'm meeting him tomorrow afternoon because he wants to speak with Carter."

"I'll come too," said Favor.

"*Nee*. It's just the two of us. No one can come. He wants to talk to Carter."

Cherish raised her eyebrows. "About what?"

"Something to do with how he used to work for him. I'm not sure, really, but this visit should be just the two of us."

"Can I get you a plate of something, Hope? Have you had enough to eat?" asked Bliss.

"I've had a bit to eat and I couldn't fit in anymore. Thanks for asking, though." She looked over at Fairfax who had just sat down with one of the Miller boys and their visitor, Adam. "I'm not staying for the singing. Fairfax and I have been told we should go home after the meeting."

"I'll stay on for the singing and bring the girls home. You'll have to go home with Levi and *Mamm.*"

"I know."

Bliss stared at Adam. She didn't want to let her chance to know him better slip by.

CHAPTER 12

IT WAS when the singing was over that Bliss's opportunity to talk to Adam came. As soon as she stood up, he was right there next to her.

"Bliss, I just wanted to let you know that I'm really sorry about Bruiser. I have apologized to Cherish. I seriously thought he was a boy. It's very hard to tell with the young. You see when you turn them over—"

"No need to go into all the details." Bliss giggled, aware that everyone could see them talking. "I'm not going to turn my bunnies over to look at that part of them. They're cute and fluffy and that's all I need to know."

"I don't want you to get into the same trouble as I did. I've had a really hard think about it and I honestly can't remember telling Cherish that Bruiser was a boy. I'm sure I said I *thought* he was a boy. She never mentioned it was important that she have a boy rabbit."

"It's okay, it worked out well."

He grinned at her. "It must've given you a shock when he had the babies. I'm glad you got him back again."

"*Her* back, and *she* had babies." Bliss corrected him with a big smile.

"Yes, her."

"It was horrible when she got away. I mean farmers shoot rabbits. I was dreadfully worried and sick every night thinking that she might be dead out there somewhere got by some wild animal or shot by some farmer."

"Yes, not many people understand rabbits."

"I do."

"I can see you like them as much as I do."

She stared into his eyes as everyone around them milled around talking to one another. "I do." This was a man Bliss could see herself with and she was so pleased Cherish was no longer interested in him.

"I wasn't sure. I wasn't sure if you liked them. I thought you were a quiet girl, but then I got your letter and saw a different side. I must say, I like that side better."

Bliss wasn't sure what he was talking about, but she liked what he was saying.

He was smiling at her, but was he smiling in a mocking way looking at all the freckles on her face? She once thought her freckles were cute, but the way Cherish spoke about them she figured maybe they weren't. All she wanted was for him to see a beautiful girl looking back at him, but did he see the same ugliness that Cherish saw? She stepped back. "I should get back to my sisters."

"No. Stay and talk a while?"

She looked around to see where they were. "They'll be going home soon."

He smiled. "They won't go without you, will they? Hey, why don't I take you home?"

This was the best outcome Bliss could've hoped for. "Okay. I'll tell them."

She went to go and he took hold of her arm. "They can find out when they come to fetch you."

"Okay." Bliss stifled a girlish giggle. That meant he was saying that he didn't want to waste a minute of their time together.

"I'd like to see your baby rabbits."

"Then you should come to the house sometime. Maybe later this week?" Now she wasn't so upset about her father and Wilma going away. It couldn't have come at a better time.

"I'd like that."

She thought fast. "My father and stepmother are going away for a few days. The girls and I are having dinner for some of our friends while they're gone. I'd love to have you join us."

"I'll be there."

"Good. I'll let you know the time and day when it gets closer."

He nodded. "Let's sit down."

They sat on the Hershberger's porch while people loaded up the long benches onto the specially made wagon that carried them to every meeting.

"Tell me about your family," Bliss said.

"I'm one of many. There are eleven of us. I'm the eldest. Five boys and six girls."

"That's nice. I was an only child until *Dat* married Wilma. Wilma has six girls, a stepdaughter and two stepsons, and a ..." She wondered how to describe what Carter was—Wilma's child she'd had out of wedlock—but then she remembered no one was supposed to talk about that. Wilma was always worried about bringing shame to the family. She'd heard that out of Wilma's mouth so often, probably at the rate of once a week since she'd joined the family.

"That's a lot. How do you cope with all that after being the only one for so long?"

Bliss smiled. "Most of them have left home now. There's only Cherish, Favor, me and Hope at home. Joy and Isaac live in a caravan on the property. They're married."

"I guessed that."

"I love being part of a big family. There's always someone to keep me company and share chores. There's always someone to speak with and I'm never lonely. It's like living with all of your best friends."

"No wonder you were so protective of Cherish. I like a loyal woman. That says a lot about the person you are."

She smiled at all the nice things he was saying. Someone must've told him good things about her.

Favor walked over to them. "We're going now, Bliss."

He stood up. "I'm taking Bliss home."

"Oh." Favor looked shocked. "Okay. I'll see you at home then." Favor turned and walked away so fast that she was nearly running.

"I think I scared her." He chuckled as he sat down again.

"You shocked her. That's because no one's taken me home before."

"I can't believe that."

They smiled at each other and she loved the way the gas lights reflected in his eyes. For good measure, she added, "I've been asked, but always said no."

"I'm glad I'm the first." He stood and offered his hand. She grabbed it and stood up. "We should go before the Hershbergers kick us out."

"I'm ready."

On the drive home, he said, "I want to see you sooner than the dinner you're having, but I've committed myself to working all this week right up until Sunday. Can I see you next week sometime?"

"Sure. I'd like that. I start my new job at a café on Tuesday of next week. It's only for four hours, but I keep telling everyone it's a start."

"It is. How about I collect you from the café?"

"*Jah*, perfect. By then I'll know when we're having that dinner." She told him the name of the café and gave him directions to get there.

When he pulled the buggy into her driveway, he said, "I'm so pleased I came back here."

"Me too. What made you decide to come back?"

"It was your letter."

"Oh, was it?"

"That's right." He stopped the buggy when they reached the house, and then turned his body to face her. "Your personality shone through your letter."

"I'm pleased I sent it. I nearly didn't."

"I'm pleased you did too. I'm so happy I've come here."

"Me too." After they exchanged smiles, she glanced at the house, and then looked back at him. "They're probably waiting for me to come inside before they go to bed."

"Most likely."

She couldn't stop herself from smiling. Before there was an awkward moment where she wouldn't know what to say next, she got out of the buggy. She stood there and said through the window, "I had a nice night."

"Me too, Bliss. Tuesday next week seems such a long way away."

Bliss had never felt so happy. She turned on her heel and headed into the house. No one had ever shown her that much attention or said such nice things to her. She opened the door and closed it behind her while listening to the rhythmical sounds of the buggy moving away.

Cherish walked up to her. "How did you get him to drive you home?"

Bliss moved past her and saw that they were alone. Everyone must've already gone to bed since there was no one in the living room and no light on in the kitchen. "He likes me, I guess."

"Really?"

She didn't like the way Cherish looked so surprised. "He as good as said so. We have a lot in common and it seems he's not bothered by my freckles and my fat."

"Hey, don't say that. You're trying to make out I said you look bad, but I didn't. I was trying to make you feel good about yourself."

"How? By pointing out all my flaws? I know I'll never

be as pretty as you are, Cherish, and I'm fine with that. A man will love me for the inside of me and not the outside of me."

"Can't he love both?"

"For people like you, *jah*, but for people like me, no. He already said my true personality came out in that letter I sent him. That's why he came back. He likes my true personality."

Cherish rubbed her head. "What? The reason he's back is because he thought … he liked what you said in the letter?"

"That's right."

Cherish was mystified. "What part of the letter?"

"He didn't say exactly, but he said he could see I was a faithful and honest person."

Cherish sighed. "I'm going to bed."

"I might stay up for a little while and make myself a cup of hot tea."

"Yeah, you do that." Cherish turned and walked up the stairs.

"Wait, Cherish," Bliss whispered from the bottom of the stairs.

Cherish hurried down to meet her. "What?"

"I kind of told Adam we were having a dinner here when *Dat* and *Mamm* were away. Would that be okay?" she whispered back.

"'Okay?' That's genius thinking."

Bliss moved closer. "And do you agree that we shouldn't mention it to them because they might not allow it?"

"I agree very much."

"I can't wait, Cherish."

"Good. Me neither." Cherish continued back up the stairs. That was Bliss's first good idea. By the time the night of the dinner came 'round, she hoped Adam would figure out he was in love with her and not Bliss. This was a total disaster. If she confessed it was she who wrote that letter, he wouldn't think she was honorable at all. Now Bliss had stars in her eyes thinking Adam loved her.

Cherish closed her bedroom door behind her. Flopping down on her bed, she decided that it wouldn't take Adam long to tire of Bliss. Then she'd be right there ready and waiting to snap him up. Maybe the dinner would come at the very right time.

CHAPTER 13

THROUGHOUT THE WHOLE WEEKEND, the Baker girls and their mother hadn't talked much. By Monday all the girls knew that Wilma and Levi were intending to go on vacation, but neither *Mamm* nor Levi had mentioned a word.

They sat down to eat an evening meal of roasted chicken. Wilma had insisted on making it herself with no help from the girls. After Levi complimented *Mamm* on the dinner, Cherish noticed the sickening smile Levi gave *Mamm*. It turned Cherish's stomach. She liked the old Levi better—the one that didn't get along so well with her mother.

Hope cleared her throat. "*Mamm*, Levi, do you have something to tell us?"

Mamm stared at Levi and then Levi spoke. "Your *mudder* and I are going away for a few days. I've been in contact with the owner of one of the biggest apple orchards in New York and he's graciously offered for me to visit his orchard so I can learn more."

"You don't need to go away for that," Favor said. "One of *Dat's* good friends is helping Florence to start her orchard from scratch. He'll help you too if you ask."

A gruff sound emanated from Levi's throat. "I'm guessing he'll want payment?"

"I don't know."

"This man's asking for nothing."

Hope said, "But you're going all that way, so isn't that costly?"

Mamm leaned forward and touched Hope's hand. "I'll be seeing Honor and Mercy too and their *bopplis.*"

Levi added, "And, all I see from Florence's orchard is dirt on level ground. I take that back. On not-so-level ground. I wouldn't like someone like that helping me." He chuckled but it came out more of a scoff. "How do we know the trees will even grow on that land? There was a reason that portion of land was discarded by your *vadder* in the first place. It's low-lying land."

Cherish said, "Florence said he knows what he's doing. You just can't stick trees in the ground and hope for the best. The ground has to be properly prepared and drainage dug. So, that's why it looks the way it does. It won't be forever."

Favor added, "*Jah,* and there might be a way to compensate for the land being low lying. If there is a way, Florence will find it."

Levi put up his hand. "I've heard enough. I don't know why you girls have to argue with everything I say. That's what we're doing and that's the end of it."

Everyone was silent for a moment before *Mamm* spoke in a meek voice repeating what she'd said earlier. "While we're there, it's not too far away from Mercy and Honor."

"That's nice, *Mamm*. You'll get to see them again," said Bliss, smiling at her stepmother.

"Can I come too?" asked Favor.

"*Nee*, I'm sorry. It's just Levi and me who are going and no one ask that again. You girls have to learn you can't get your way by nagging."

"So we're gonna be left with no supervision from anyone? Because I could have one of my pen pals to stay. Someone older and responsible. You said I could have someone come to stay, Levi. This might be the perfect time."

He put down his knife and fork and clasped his hands on the table in front of him. "It's not the perfect time at all, Favor. Not when we're away. You will be allowed to have a pen pal come to stay at a future time. Your *mudder* and I have discussed it, but it has to be at the right time that suits Wilma and me."

Favor sat there in silence pushing the food around on her plate with a fork.

"Of course we shouldn't need to be supervised, we're all adults here. You should go away more often. We can handle everything here and do what needs to be done in the orchard," said Hope.

Levi picked up his fork and stabbed a golden roasted potato. "The orchard can look after itself for a couple of weeks. There's still some pruning to do, but I'll leave that to you girls." He turned to his daughter. "Bliss, you can organize that. If you can fit it around all those hours you've now got at the café."

Bliss's eyes bugged out. "Okay."

Cherish didn't say anything. Of all the girls he could ask, he chose the one who knew nothing about apple trees.

Hope leaned forward. "A couple of weeks? That's how long you're going for?"

"That's right. Including the traveling time," Levi said.

"You'll both have a wonderful time." Bliss smiled at her father.

"It's mostly work," said Levi.

Either way, Cherish was pleased to have a lovely break from chores. They wouldn't do a thing until the day before they came home. Cherish was looking forward to that and she was sure she could get the other girls to agree to doing nothing. The only problem she could foresee was Joy. There had to be a way to get rid of Joy and Isaac from the property. Even though they lived in the caravan behind the barn, that was way too close. Cherish cleared her throat. "And I've heard Ada and Samuel are also going away, so you're going away with them ... together?"

"That's right," said Levi. "We're going together."

"Do they have someone to look after their place? I'm sure Joy and Isaac would love to help them out."

Slowly, Levi nodded. "That might be a good idea, Cherish. I'll mention it to Samuel and Ada tomorrow. They'll be here in the morning to organize the travel plans."

Cherish was pleased to hear that. If they could get rid of Joy, then Favor, Hope, Bliss, and she would have a vacation themselves without their mother and stepfather and fussy older sister watching over them. Then they'd have that dinner with their friends, but they couldn't make plans until her parents were well and truly gone and Joy and Isaac safely out of the way at Ada and Samuel's house.

Feeling someone watching her Cherish looked up. It was Bliss. They exchanged a secretive smile, both thinking about that dinner.

CHAPTER 14

THE NEXT MORNING, Cherish had to stop herself from helping her plan along. She was tempted to go to Joy's caravan and inform her Ada and Samuel might need someone to stay at their house. The problem was, Joy wasn't stupid and if she knew Cherish wanted her to go to Ada's, she'd figure out why. No, this was one thing Cherish had to let go of.

When Ada and Samuel arrived, Cherish waited in her room for a few minutes. Then she crept onto the stairs and stayed out of sight. With her excellent hearing, she could hear every word that was said as they sat at the large dining table figuring out the plans of where they would stay and such.

Half an hour later, after many decisions had been made, her stepfather spoke. "Have you found someone to look after your place while you're gone?"

"I was going to ask Joy and Isaac," Ada said.

Cherish clapped her hands with delight. Then, hearing nothing from the adults, she quickly ran up the stairs so they wouldn't know she'd been listening. This was perfect. It was all meant to be because, even if she hadn't planted that seed in Levi's head, Ada had been thinking about it anyway.

She took out pen and paper and sitting on the windowsill, she wrote down all the food they'd need for the dinner they'd have. They'd have so much fun with no adults there.

Movement from below caught her eye. It was her mother and Ada. The only reason they'd be outside was that they were heading to talk with Joy. There would be no reason for Joy to refuse them. She'd be doing Ada and Samuel a favor and she and Isaac would have a house to stay in by themselves.

JOY WAS MAKING the bed when she heard someone approaching. She opened the door and saw *Mamm* and Ada.

"Hello. I didn't know you were here, Ada."

"Is this where you and Isaac have been hiding, Joy?"

Joy giggled. "Come in and take a look."

"Thank you, I will." Ada stepped up into the caravan and took a look around.

"This is where we sleep. This is our little kitchen and that's where we sit to eat our meals. Oh, and behind that door is the world's smallest bathroom."

"There's everything here you'd need. It's much bigger than it looks from the outside."

"It serves its purpose. Would you like to sit down? I can make you hot tea or *kaffe.*"

"We've just had hot tea at the *haus*, but I will sit for a moment. I've got something to ask you."

"Okay."

Once they were seated, Ada said, "Joy, would you stay at our *haus* while we go away with your *mudder*? It'll only be for two weeks or a few days longer."

"We'd love that. I'm sure Isaac would agree."

"There will be just a few animals to feed. If you can stop by sometime before we leave on Friday I'll show you what needs to be done."

"Perfect, I can't wait. It'll be a taste of having our own place."

"It will give me peace of mind that someone is staying on the property and looking after the animals."

"Can I bring Goldie?"

"Of course you can."

"*Wunderbaar.*"

Cherish had crept up and was listening just outside the door. Her plan had worked perfectly. She popped her head into the caravan. "What's everyone talking about?"

"Ada has just asked Joy to stay at her place while she goes away."

"Truly? I would've done it, Ada."

Ada looked at her. "Joy is older and more responsible and Isaac will be there to help keep everything going."

"Okay, but it doesn't seem fair."

Ada chuckled. "Nothing seems fair to you, Cherish."

Cherish pouted so they wouldn't know she was secretly pleased. She sat down sideways on the doorstep, facing inward. "You'll have such fun on your trip away. You'll get to see the *bopplis,* Ada."

"I know and I'm looking forward to it. It's because of me that Mercy married Stephen."

Cherish smiled. *"Denke* for matching them together. And it was because of that—"

"Jonathon and Honor were just a natural progression after that. And Matthew is the perfect answer as a husband for one of you *schweschders."*

Matthew was the younger brother of Stephen and Jonathon. "Oh, you think so?"

Cherish made a face. Everyone knew that Matthew had a big crush on Hope, but that was never going to happen since Hope and Fairfax were practically engaged. "I think that he can find his own *fraa* from his own community."

Ada raised her eyebrows. "His mother told me that he likes one of you."

"He likes Hope," Joy said. "There's no secret about that. Everyone knows it, but Hope only has eyes for Fairfax."

"Joy!" Cherish was shocked. That was supposed to be kept quiet.

"Do you think that your *mudder* hasn't told me about Fairfax and Hope, Cherish? It's no good trying to keep a secret from me."

"Ada won't say anything. She's not a gossip," *Mamm* said.

"That's right. Wilma tells me everything because she knows it won't go any further. If word got out, people might think that she's the only reason he's joining us."

"That's between them and *Gott*, it's not for me to comment about," said Joy.

Cherish leaned her back against the door frame. "When are you leaving?"

"At the end of the week. We're hoping for Friday, but we're not certain which day. It depends when we can get the cheapest travel tickets."

"We've left Samuel and Levi to make the calls. We're staying with our sisters and brothers where we can."

"Sounds exciting," Cherish said. "You'll have such a good time. I wish I was going too."

"You'll still have to do all the chores. Everything must carry along the same as though Levi and I were still here."

"Of course it will, *Mamm,* don't you worry about a thing."

"I hope I can trust you girls, or I won't be going away again and there will be severe punishments." Wilma all but shook her finger at her. Her stern face served the same purpose.

"You don't need to say those things, *Mamm.* We will carry on as usual. I don't know why you'd even consider for a moment that we wouldn't. I guess with Joy gone, Hope will be in charge."

"*Gut,* someone sensible in charge," Ada said.

Joy giggled. "They'll be okay. It'll do them good to be by themselves."

"I hope you're right, Joy," *Mamm* said.

"Have a little more confidence," Cherish said.

"No more animals." *Mamm* pointed at Cherish. "Is that understood?"

"*Jah,* perfectly. I do think we have enough of those."

"Because if I come back to find more animals, I won't care if they've been someone's presents or not, they're going back to where they came from."

"I hear you. Now I have to get ready for work." Cherish stood up, said her goodbyes and hurried back to the house.

CHAPTER 15

As ARRANGED, Hope and Fairfax met outside of Carter and Florence's property and then they walked in to see them together.

"How are you doing?" Hope noticed Fairfax looked tired. His face was pale and he had dark circles under his eyes. He looked far worse than he had the day before.

"Every muscle in my body is aching and so is my head. Milking takes hours and it's twice a day, and they're totally inconvenient hours. Firstly, before the sun comes up. Before this, I wasn't an early riser. I thought six was early. Nope, we're up at four and out the door."

Hope couldn't help laughing at his sad face. "Oh, I don't mean to laugh, I'm sorry. Is it that bad?"

"Words can't express. I've only been there a few days and I don't know how much more I can handle."

"'Handle?' What do you mean by that?"

"I don't know. I really don't know. It's an inhuman experience. And it's only been a few days and I miss not being able to play video games and watch things on TV.

That's the way I chill out, and now I don't know what to do to wind down and I look up at the ceiling and that's it."

She had hoped that praying or nightly Bible readings with the Millers might have helped him 'wind down.' "It's a big change. You'll get used to it in time."

"Maybe I will."

Hope didn't know what to say. At the meeting yesterday, he wasn't complaining this much, but she could tell he was hiding something. Was he going to quit without even being there a full week? "I don't know what to say, Fairfax," she said as they strolled to Florence and Carter's cottage.

"Neither do I. Perhaps my body will toughen up. I already thought it was tough, but I'd never done anything like this before. It's worse than mucking out stables every day. Every night I go to sleep with the smell of cow dung in my nostrils. There's more things they can do without the use of electricity. There are machines, that I'm sure the bishop would approve of."

"The Millers would know all that, but choose not to. I wouldn't mention anything to them. They'd still see you as an outsider and they wouldn't appreciate any suggestions."

"I know what you mean. That's why I've kept quiet."

"Good."

"I'll just keep going, and going, and going until I've done my three months internship."

She smiled at him, but she was disappointed that he hadn't mentioned anything about God or that he was looking forward to taking the instructions. After all, that was the purpose of him joining them—leaving the outside world and all that it represented. Now he sounded like he was regretting it. She couldn't get her hopes up just yet. Hope had been dreaming about their wedding and what their life would be like but now she knew nothing was secure, nothing was a certainty. All she could do was wait and see what happened.

"I've told my parents about you and they want to meet you. They asked if you'd come to dinner one night," he whispered when they were nearly at the cottage.

Hope knew that was a good sign. She'd never met them. Only seen his mother by accident when Mrs. Jenkins had mistaken her for Cherish. "Of course I will. When?"

"Wednesday night."

"Okay. I'll look forward to it." They walked up the porch stairs and Hope knocked on the door.

Florence opened the door with the baby in her arms.

"Wow, she's so much bigger than when I last saw her," Hope said.

"She has put on a little weight. Hello, Fairfax."

"Hi, Florence."

"Look at you in your Amish clothing—plain folks' clothes."

He looked down at himself. "I never thought this would happen, but I never thought I'd meet anyone like Hope."

Florence stepped back to allow them in. "Come inside." She walked into the living room and they followed. She passed the baby to Hope and they sat down.

Carter came down from upstairs to join them. "Look at you two. That looks like a fine picture. Baby makes three."

Everyone laughed. "Well, maybe we'll be a couple in a year or so," Fairfax said giving Hope a little more confidence.

"Yes, at the moment it's *borrowed* baby makes three."

"One day we'll have our own," said Fairfax.

Hope couldn't keep the smile from her face.

"So you really did it, Fairfax?" Carter sat down on the couch with them.

"I did. The family hosting me are the Millers. They have a dairy farm. I never knew what hard work was like."

"I was too easy on you, then," Carter said with a laugh.

"Maybe. And my parents, too. I've been meaning to have a more in-depth talk with you about leaving you so suddenly. I know you were probably hoping to rely on me when my parents leave for Florida."

"You don't owe me any explanations. You have to do what's right for you. I have heard dairy farms are tough work, though, even with modern equipment."

"They don't have equipment at all."

"Is that the only place you could've stayed?"

"I don't know. That's where the bishop put me. I think he put me at the very worst place, at least from what I've heard. I think he's testing me because he knows I'm involved with Hope and so he wants to make sure I join for the right reasons."

"I think you're exactly right," Florence said. "It sounds exactly like something he would do."

"I've just got to make it through the next three months."

"You'll do it," said Carter.

"Congratulations on the baby," Fairfax said.

"Thank you," said Florence. "Congratulations on your becoming Amish."

"Well, I'm not Amish yet, until I go through the instructions and get baptized, but I'm well on the way."

"We have to kind of lay low with our relationship until then," Hope said. "It's on hold."

"I think that's best," said Florence. "We don't want those tongues wagging. Would you like a glass of lemonade? Carter made some fresh this morning."

Hope could barely take her eyes from the baby. "I'm okay thanks."

"I'd like some," said Fairfax.

Carter stood. "Come with me. I'll get you that lemonade and we'll leave these two to talk."

Fairfax stood too and when the men left the room, Florence whispered. "How's it going, for real?"

"I'm not sure. I really don't know if he'll make it through."

"Of course he will. He's not the type of man to start something and not finish it. You're his whole world, Hope. I can see it in his eyes."

"Really?"

"Yes. The bishop is testing him, I'm sure of it. The last *Englisher* who'd been sent to live with the Millers left before two weeks were up."

Hope smiled and looked down at the sleeping baby. "Do you have a name for her yet?"

"We do. It's Iris Eleanor."

"Oh, after *Mamm's schweschder*."

"That's right, and my mother."

"That's *wunderbaar*, and you said you weren't going to name her after anyone."

"I know, but it seems right."

"It does. I agree." Hope stared down at Iris in wonder. How long would it be before she had her own baby—hers and Fairfax's? Would their baby be this beautiful? "She's so lovely, Florence. If she were mine I'd look at her all day. I'd get nothing else done."

Florence giggled. "She is amazing. Babies are such miracles. She's such a gift. I feel complete now. We have a real family."

Several minutes later, Fairfax and Carter walked back into the room. "I'll need to go now, Hope. They'll miss me if I'm gone any longer. You can stay here."

"No, it's okay. I should get back home, too."

After the couple said their goodbyes, they walked back to the front gate. "I guess I'll see you on Friday night."

"Yes. We'll have an early dinner at six. I've already arranged it with Mom."

"Okay, that sounds great."

"I think of you every moment, Hope. Especially when I close my eyes to go to sleep. I imagine what it's going to be like when we're married and can be together. I'll get my own horse and buggy as soon as I can and we can save up and get a house."

"*Jah*, and it doesn't have to be something grand. Something small to start with."

"Believe me, it will be nothing grand since my parents sold my inheritance rather than passing it down to me."

"Whatever it is, it'll be ours and we can build our future and our family."

"Am I allowed to kiss you?"

Hope looked around. "Just quickly."

He gave her a quick kiss on the lips and then smiled. And he got into his buggy and drove away. Hope started off walking home to the next-door property. As she walked she realized she'd felt too scared to even imagine what life would be like if she married Fairfax. Would the test of the dairy be too much for him? The bishop *was* testing him, that was for sure.

She couldn't rest easy until they were in front of the bishop and he was marrying them.

CHAPTER 16

HOPE WAS surprised Wilma and Levi were allowing her to go to Fairfax's parents' house for dinner. It seemed they'd accepted her future with him already. It was just as the sun was going down that she headed away from her home, and walked through the orchard and met Fairfax at the fence line near the cottage where he used to live. She was nervous about meeting his parents, but when she saw him, she knew it would be all right. By the time she slipped through the fence wires, he was right there.

They hugged each other for more than a moment.

"My folks are looking forward to seeing you."

"I'm looking forward to meeting them too. I'm scared, though."

"Don't be anxious. They feel like that about meeting you, too."

"Are they angry with me?"

He put his arm around her as they walked. "Why would they be?"

"I don't know, for stealing you away or something."

"You didn't steal me away. This is what I want to do with my life. It feels right to be with you in the community. It's a life worth living."

That was just what she wanted to hear. "Have you told your parents that?"

"Not in so many words, but they know."

"How will they know if you don't tell them?"

"We're close, but we don't talk about feelings and stuff. We mainly talk about more day to day things. They made the decision to move to Florida without talking to me about it until after it was a done deal. At least I talked to them before I made this decision."

"What do you think they'll ask me?"

"I don't know, but whatever it is, just answer it and don't worry. Just be honest."

"Of course I'll be honest. I'm just a little worried about the questions they might ask me."

"Relax, I'll be there. They're nice people."

"They must be nice since they're your parents."

He grinned. "That's right."

"Your mother saw me with you once and thought I was Cherish. Do you remember?"

"I do and I didn't even know where she'd met Cherish." He laughed.

"I was worried that you liked Cherish—she tried to use her charms on Stephen, my older sister's husband. That was before they were married."

"You'll never have to worry about that sort of thing with me. You're the only woman I see."

She was pleased to hear it, but just then she looked up

and saw how close the house was. Her nerves kicked in again. She was only moments away from meeting his parents.

Fairfax walked in the front door holding Hope's hand. "Hello, anyone home?"

His mother walked out followed by his father.

"Hope, it's lovely to meet you." His mother hurried over and hugged her.

Hope wasn't expecting her to be so warm and friendly, and then his father smiled at her and reached out his hand and Hope shook it. "I'm pleased to meet you both."

She could see where Fairfax got his good looks. Both the parents were attractive and looked young for parents of someone Fairfax's age. "Dinner smells nice."

"I thought I'd do my best because Fairfax told me what a good cook you are."

"I'm okay. Nothing special."

"I'm Nola and this is Warren."

"Good. I won't call you Mr. and Mrs. Jenkins, then, if that's what you prefer."

"Please don't," Warren said. "Come this way, Hope. I've got some things you need to see."

She walked with him and glanced back at Fairfax who shrugged his shoulders as though he didn't know what his father was talking about. When she got into the living room she saw books.

"Oh Dad, not the photos," Fairfax said when he saw them too.

"I'm sure Hope would like to see how cute you were as a baby. Wouldn't you Hope?"

"I sure would."

"And we've got photos of him at all his milestones."

"There are way too many photos of me. It's not normal."

"Correct me if I'm wrong, Hope, but your community doesn't take photos and you don't like being photographed?"

"That's right. We don't. They would be good to look back on, though." Hope sat on the couch and then Nola and Warren sat either side of her while Fairfax sat opposite.

"Do we really have to do this?" Fairfax grumbled. "I thought we were here for dinner."

"Don't worry, you'll get fed," Nola said. "Hope wants to see them."

"Yes I do."

"Hope, you're the first girl he's ever brought here for dinner." Warren grinned.

"Oh, come on, Dad. You're making me sound like a complete—"

"Actually you're wrong, Dear. Hope's the only girl he brought home, for dinner or otherwise."

His father grinned widely.

Hope laughed at Fairfax when he slid down in his seat, putting his hand on his head with embarrassment.

Fairfax's mother opened the first album, which was full of his baby photos.

"Oh, you still look like you, Fairfax," Hope said looking at the cute and chubby baby wrapped in a blue blanket.

"That's right. He hasn't changed much at all," said Nola.

"Yeah, I'm about six feet tall now though."

"But I can still tell it's you. You've got the same eyes and the same shape face."

Fairfax rolled his eyes. "How far away is dinner, Mom?"

"It's all ready. We're just having a look at the photos first."

After they'd shown Hope all the photos, Nola said, "I'm glad you've come, Hope, because I've got a few questions."

"Sure, what is it?"

"We're moving away shortly, so is Fairfax allowed to visit us? We'll be in Florida."

"Yes. People choose to separate from their families when they join us, but they certainly don't have to do that. I mean, he probably couldn't live with you again."

"I'm too old to live with them anyway," Fairfax said.

"You were up until a year ago, son."

"Yeah, well that was too long to stay. No offense or anything."

"And can we visit him?" Nola asked.

"Sure. Of course."

"And you really have no electricity or modern conveniences?" his mother asked.

"Mom, you know the answer to that. We've been living alongside the Amish all these years. Don't ask questions that you know the answer to."

"I'm curious, that's all."

"It's perfectly alright. I want to answer your questions as fully as I can. Did Fairfax explain the process he's going through?"

Husband and wife looked at each other and then nodded.

"He did. It's going to take us some time to get used to this. He might've been thinking about it for a while, but it came suddenly to us."

"I understand. It's not … It would be a big adjustment to make."

"You don't exactly look the picture of health, Fairfax. What's going on?"

"I'm fine. I just haven't been sleeping. Once I get a good sleep, things will be different. I'm doing much harder physical work than I've ever done before."

His father leaned over and slapped him on the back. "Good, and that won't hurt you. So where do you both see yourself in five years?"

Hope didn't know what to say. "I'd have to let Fairfax answer that."

Both mother and father stared at Fairfax.

"Married to Hope with a couple of young kids. And a guestroom for when you come to visit."

"Is that what you think, Hope?" Warren asked.

"Yes. That sounds good to me."

"So are you really going to do this, son?"

"It's done, Dad. I am doing it."

"But you can always change your mind, can't you? You're not locked in?" his mother asked.

"Anyone can change their mind along the way, it's not that it's locked in or anything," Hope said, "but once we're married, I'm hoping he won't change his mind."

"You don't have to worry about that, Hope. I'm fully committed to you and to your community."

She smiled at him, quite pleased he'd said that in front of his folks. It made it all seem real.

"And how would you support yourself?" Warren asked.

"We hope to have an orchard one day. Much like this one. There are many ways we can make money out of an orchard."

"Everyone ready for dinner?"

"Yes, please," said Fairfax. "I'm always ready for dinner."

"It'll be a moment. Would you like to help me in the kitchen, Hope?"

"Sure."

Hope left the men, guessing that now the real questions would start and she wasn't wrong. As soon as they were in the kitchen the serious conversation started.

"It's a little upsetting for me because he's my only son and he's not coming with us to Florida like we thought he would."

"I can imagine it would be upsetting. He told me he always said he was never going there with you. He doesn't want to live there."

"I know that now. At least I know he'll be in good hands. I'm so pleased he found you before we left. It's always such a worry for parents. He's always been a good boy. He's always been a loner and has never really gotten along too well with other people."

"That's surprising to hear you say that. He seems to get along with everybody."

"Maybe he does. Maybe that's why he belongs in your community if he gets along well with everybody there. He never got along with his peer group. He didn't have too many friends in school—that kind of thing."

"I had no idea."

"It's true, and I guess we'll have many grandchildren?"

Hope put her hand to her mouth and giggled. "I certainly hope so."

"Yes, that's good. We can come back and visit the grandchildren. Oh, Hope, I can't wait for that day."

"When are you leaving for Florida?"

"In a few months. We've bought a condo in a new development. It'll be ready on September one."

"Sounds great."

"And where will you live?"

"I'm not too sure yet. We could possibly live at my folks' place. That's what my older sister Joy did—is still doing—with her husband. They're actually staying in a caravan that was towed onto the property so they could have their own space."

"That sounds like an excellent idea."

"It's a little cramped, but it's just the two of them so far and they're happy with it."

"I'm sure you two will work things out your own way."

"We will. We've got a lot of family support and it's good to know that Fairfax has your support. That truly makes a difference."

"He'll always have that. No matter what he decides to do. Wherever he goes in life and whatever he does. It's his journey not ours."

"That's a good way to look at things."

"That's the only way we can look at things. We had

him late in life and even though he's everything to us, we realize we have our own life to live and we have to do what is good for us as well."

"Oh, I didn't think you had him late in life. You and your husband look so young."

Nola smiled. "Thank you, but we're retirement age. I'm pleased to know we don't look it."

"Not at all."

"The table's set. Help me carry the bowls to the table?"

"Sure."

When the dinner was over, Fairfax made his excuses for them to leave fairly soon. He had the borrowed horse and buggy waiting to take Hope home.

His parents hugged Hope when they were leaving, and she was relieved that they liked her and approved of Fairfax's plans.

"That went well," Fairfax said as he drove away from the house.

"It did. They're so nice."

"They're okay."

"Saturday night we're having people to the *haus*. *Mamm* and Levi are going away and … will you be able to come?"

"Yeah, I don't see why not. Saturday night you say?"

"*Jah.*"

"I'll be there."

"Cherish and Favor are organizing it."

Fairfax chuckled. "Should I be worried?"

"Probably."

When Fairfax got to Hope's house, she gave him a quick kiss on his cheek before she got out of the buggy and headed to the house. Every time she left him she felt like she was leaving a small part of herself behind. Soon, they'd be married and then her real life would start.

CHAPTER 17

FINALLY THE DAY came that all the girls had been waiting on. It was early Friday morning and their parents were leaving for their vacation.

"The car's here, *Mamm!*" Cherish screeched at the top of her lungs. She couldn't wait to be alone in the house. Joy and Isaac had left yesterday to stay the night at Ada and Samuel's house so they'd have an early start with feeding the animals while the older couple got ready to go. When the car came to a halt, the girls stood on the porch watching them leave. Their hired car had already collected Ada and Samuel. Samuel sat in the front seat because of his bad leg.

Levi put their bags in the trunk and then there were hugs all around before Wilma and Levi got in the car.

When they were halfway down the driveway, Cherish noticed Bliss and Favor were upset. "What's wrong with you two? They're coming back you know."

"Cherish, we won't see them for so long."

"And how is that a bad thing?" Cherish laughed,

hoping that might encourage them to see the more positive side.

Then Hope walked toward the barn. "I'll see everyone later. I'm off to work," she called over her shoulder.

"Wait. I'll drive you and collect you this afternoon."

"*Denke*, Cherish, but Levi told us to use the horses sparingly."

"I would, but I've got to invite everybody to our party tomorrow night."

"Party? I thought it was a dinner."

"Ooh, you're right, party sounds bad. Let's just call it a barbecue. Relax, it's nothing bad. We're just having a little get together with the young people. And isn't it about time we did something like that?"

"I don't know."

"It'll be a chance for you to see Fairfax again."

"I don't know if it's a good idea. Who... I mean, what adults will be here to supervise?"

"You heard them, we are all adults. That's why they left us. If they thought we were children, they wouldn't have left us."

"I've already invited Fairfax. I hope nothing goes wrong. *Mamm* and Levi didn't say we could have people here."

"And neither did they say that we couldn't. It'll be fun," Cherish insisted.

"I'll come with you, Cherish," said Bliss, hurrying over to her.

"Me too," said Favor. "I don't want to be here on my own."

"Okay. You two are hitching the buggy if you want to come."

Once the buggy was hitched, they all got in. Halfway down the driveway, Favor said, "It feels weird with them gone."

"*Jah*, good weird," Cherish said. "We're just gonna have such fun tomorrow

We'll have to buy a lot of food. I have some money I'm putting toward it and I've got the emergency money they left us."

Hope groaned. "Cherish, that was for *emergencies*. You can't use it just to entertain people."

"It will be an emergency if people arrive and there's no food."

"That's right. We have to feed them something," Bliss said. "How many are coming?"

"I don't know. As many as want to come."

"Sounds like a good idea to me," said Favor. "And should we invite Joy and Isaac as well?"

"*Nee*, Favor. It's kind of a secret barbecue. Joy would just be looking over our shoulders the whole time. I might invite some of the workers at the café."

"I really don't think that's a good idea, to invite *Englishers*. Let's just stick to people from the community, shall we?" Hope said, just as they stopped at the B&B.

"Okay, you're right," Cherish agreed.

Hope got out. "*Denke*, and I finish at two remember. Don't be late."

"I'll be here. Don't worry."

When they got back onto the road, Favor said, "Maybe

she's right, Cherish. I know you're just telling Hope that to keep her happy."

"No! No one is gonna be the boss of me anymore. I'll turn around and take you back home if you don't like it, Favor. You can stay in your room when the party's on."

Favor frowned. "I'm just worried about the people you're inviting."

"Well you don't have to be. Everything will be fine. Stop being such a worrier. They'll all be responsible people. Let's just stop the worrying and start enjoying ourselves, shall we? We'll invite people today and tomorrow morning we'll go out and buy all the food."

"That sounds good, Cherish. Favor will stop worrying, won't you?" Bliss turned around from the front seat to look at Favor.

"Jah. Okay."

"Not a word to anyone's parents. We'll have to tell everyone we invite. We don't want this getting back to *Mamm* and Levi."

CHAPTER 18

THAT NIGHT, Levi and Wilma were having dinner with Mercy and Honor, and both of their young families. They each had a baby. Ada and Samuel were having dinner with Stephen and Jonathon's parents to allow Wilma and Levi time to catch up with the girls and their husbands.

Mercy and Honor's babies were fast asleep in the living room while the adults sat around the large kitchen table having their evening meal. Mercy sat across from Wilma and Wilma's new husband. She didn't consider Levi a stepfather because she was an adult and no longer lived at home. No, he was Wilma's husband. It was odd that her mother married again and at their wedding she'd been upset about it. She hid it from everyone. Only her husband knew how upset she was. She shared all her secret thoughts and feelings with Stephen.

Mercy stared at Levi from under her lashes as he sat at her dinner table with Honor and Honor's husband, Jonathon. She didn't know Levi well, but from what her sisters had told her in their letters, she wasn't impressed.

Even if she wanted to like him, how could she? She glanced at Honor and knew from the expression on her face she was thinking the exact same thing.

Stephen broke the ice since no one had spoken after everyone opened their eyes after their silent prayer of thanks for the food.

"I know you like jokes, Levi, so I've been saving them up for you." Stephen laughed before he even began.

"Here we go again," said Jonathon.

"I've been finding some jokes for you too," Levi said, grinning. "I'll let you go first."

"Okay. You'll find these jokes 'a peeling,' since they're about fruit. If you have any problem with what I'm about to tell you please 'lettuce' know."

Everyone chuckled. Mercy was confused as to why people were laughing. He hadn't even started yet. "Why's everyone laughing."

Jonathon said. "Lettuce know. Let us know."

Mercy shrugged. "Let us know. So what?" She turned to her husband. "That doesn't make sense. You said the jokes were about fruit not vegetables."

Stephen patted her arm. "It's okay. Mercy doesn't like my jokes, but I yam what I yam. Mercy's the apple of my eye. I couldn't have 'picked' a better *fraa.*"

Mercy drew her eyebrows together. "Start the jokes now, Stephen, everyone's waiting."

"Okay, Mercy. Here goes. What did the apple tree say to the farmer?" He looked around and no one said anything. "Stop picking on me. Here's another. Why are bananas never lonely?"

"Because they're found in bunches," Jonathon answered, shaking his head.

"That's right." Stephen chuckled. "Shall I continue?"

"Please do," said Wilma.

"What's worse than finding a worm in your apple? Finding half a worm in your apple!"

When everyone chuckled, Stephen said, "Your turn, Levi."

Levi patted his mouth with a napkin, and cleared his throat. "My jokes are about building. What did one wall say to the other?" He didn't wait for anyone to guess. "Meet you at the corner. What nails do builders hate hammering? Fingernails. Here's a measuring joke. Why can't your nose be more than twelve inches long?"

"I know this one," said Stephen. "You gave it away by saying it was a measuring joke. Your nose can't be twelve inches long because then it would be a foot."

Everyone laughed except for Mercy. "Is that it with the jokes now? Are we done?"

"I think so," said Stephen. "Unless you have more, Levi?"

Levi shook his head looking pleased with himself.

"I heard one," said *Mamm*. "It's the only one I know. Don't tell secrets in the garden. The potatoes have eyes, the beanstalk, and the corn has ears."

Levi gave a low chuckle. "I didn't know that one. You were keeping it from me."

"I was saving it up for today. I know Stephen likes a joke or two."

Mercy was thankful Stephen was trying his best. He knew how she felt about Levi.

Marriage was just like Mercy had thought it would be. She had a permanent best friend and someone with whom to share all her private thoughts. He was always there, always in her corner. And he was a wonderful father. *Gott* had heard her prayers and answered them better than she could ever have hoped.

Mercy looked over at Jonathon, Honor's husband. He was normally outgoing and outspoken, but not today. He'd sat in silence for most of the dinner, and that was probably the most awkward thing of all. Even though she never understood jokes and was mildly annoyed by them, they had served to break the ice.

Jonathon finally spoke again, "And how long do you intend to be here?"

"Here, only a couple of days, but away from home, more like two weeks at the very most," Levi said.

Mercy and Stephen's dog burst into the room and started jumping up on Levi's leg.

"Oh, I'm sorry. Get him Stephen."

Stephen jumped up and took hold of his collar. "I'm sorry. He's just overly friendly, that's a problem. He's nearly seven but he acts like a pup. I'll put him out."

"I'm sorry about that," Mercy said to Levi as Stephen led the dog out.

"No harm done," said Wilma. "At home, Goldie and Caramel are continually running about the house causing me stress. Well, that's in the past now I suppose since Goldie is not allowed in the *haus* any longer because he wants to eat Bliss's rabbit."

Stephen sat back down. "You've allowed her to have a rabbit?"

"We have."

"A *rabbit* of all things?" Stephen asked.

Mercy leaned in and whispered, "Don't go on about it."

"*Mamm,* you are getting soft." Honor chuckled. "When I wanted to get a rabbit when I was six, you said that they were pests and vermin."

"They do a lot of damage if they're not contained, I can tell you that," said Levi.

"I still believe that, Honor, but when Cherish bought the rabbit as a birthday gift for Bliss, that made things a lot more difficult."

Jonathon threw his head back and laughed. "Cherish! I might have known she would be behind it all."

Wilma nodded. "*Jah,* it's true. I don't know what to do with that girl."

"Don't worry. I hear she'll be out of the house when she's old enough, heading to Dagmar's farm. She writes about it all the time in her letters," Honor said.

"Well we can only hope," said Wilma, which made everyone giggle.

"We will miss her when she goes," said Levi, almost convincingly.

"And how's the orchard coming along, Levi?" Stephen asked as he served himself some more mashed potatoes.

"That's why we are here—part of the reason. We are visiting an orchard in New Paltz. It's two hours drive from here. We've hired a car. The owner of the orchard has kindly offered to teach me a few things."

"You had to go all the way for that, when Florence is next door and would love to help you?" Honor asked.

"Florence doesn't know that much," said Wilma. "She's had to ask for help herself."

Honor sighed, "But that's only because she's starting one fresh. She knows what to do regarding harvest and pruning and all that. She's getting expert help from the ground up."

Levi put down his knife and fork and held up his hands. "This is what pruning does."

Everyone looked at his red raw hands.

"It's hard if you're not used to the work. I'm guessing a pair of gloves would've come in handy?" Mercy said.

"Well, maybe. Anyway, that's why we're here."

"Now I can't stop thinking about Florence," Honor said. "I can't wait to see her *boppli.*"

"I always think of Florence. I'm so glad she's a mother. She'd make such a good mother. She did a very good job of being second mother to all of us girls."

"Her *boppli* is delightful and so small. I only wish we could get to see more of her."

"Well you can't," said Levi. "She left the community and best we stay clear."

"I know," said Wilma wistfully as she cut a piece of chicken. "She's still my *dochder.*"

"*Jah,* but she made her choice."

Jonathon smiled. "I agree with you, Levi. She's left the community. She should be glad that you even talk to her."

The two men exchanged smiles.

Mercy glared at Jonathon. He'd never gotten along with Florence. Florence didn't trust him and that was the main reason. Jonathon and Honor had run away together and Florence had to enlist the closest person with a car to help get her back, and that person had been Carter. It was no wonder Florence had her reservations about Jonathon. Mercy perfectly understood it. There was no reason for Jonathon to talk in a negative way about Florence. It was mean. From what Levi said just now, it was clear he didn't get along with Florence any better than he got along with his other stepchildren.

"I think it's nice that you still talk with Florence." Mercy said to Wilma. When Wilma didn't reply, Mercy knew she should've kept quiet, but she just couldn't. Someone had to stand up for her big sister. "I'll visit when I go there," she added before popping a piece of chicken into her mouth.

"Well what do you have to say about that?" Levi stared at Stephen.

Stephen put his fork down. "Well, it's not just a person, Levi. You should know how close the girls are to Florence. They're sisters. They love each other and they have a bond. A bond that cannot be broken just because one left the community. I agree that—"

"I see there's a line that she's crossed over," snapped Levi.

Mercy kept quiet, but from what Wilma had just said, Wilma had visited her. Otherwise, how could she have seen the baby?

"We have lemon pie with meringue for dessert," said Honor, changing the subject.

"I love lemon pie," said Wilma.

"I know, that's why we made it."

"I just wish you girls were closer."

"When the *bopplis* are older we can visit more," said Honor.

"I know, and we'll keep visiting as much as we can too, won't we, Levi?"

"You can if you want to. I will be occupied with the orchard."

"And who's looking after it now?" asked Mercy.

"I've left the girls to do the last of the pruning. I'm sure they'll do a good job. Cherish seems to know what she's doing more so than the others. I left Bliss in charge because Bliss is older."

"Yes, out of all the girls I remember Cherish was the one who'd follow *Dat* and Florence about. She had to pick up some knowledge when she was out there annoying them," Mercy said.

"She has a job at the coffee shop now," Levi told everyone.

"Levi is getting all the girls to get outside jobs. He said it'll be good for them to work outside the home and get to know what it's like to work for someone else. He said working for the orchard or at the roadside stall made them lazy."

"Yes, we've heard all about it through their letters," Honor said.

"I'm looking forward to visiting the orchard," said Levi. "It specializes in cider."

"Is it organic?" asked Stephen.

"*Jah,* and they grow for taste not appearance, so I guess I'm not going to follow exactly what they say."

Mercy could see what the girls said about him was true. He wasn't even going to follow what the expert said even though he had traveled nearly a day and a half to get there. It seemed that Levi thought he knew better than everybody about everything. That annoyed Mercy.

At that moment, Matthew—Stephen and Jonathon's younger brother—burst into the kitchen, startling everyone.

CHAPTER 19

"Sorry I didn't knock," said Mathew as he stared at everyone sitting around the dinner table. "I heard you were over here Mr. and Mrs. Baker. I'm sorry, I mean Mr. and Mrs. Bruner. I heard you were here and I thought I'd stop by and say hello."

"Sit down, Matthew, and I'll get a plate for you."

"No need, Mercy. I've already eaten. I'll just sit here and visit while everyone eats."

"How are you, Matthew?" Levi asked.

Mercy had heard how Levi had asked Matthew to leave his house. He'd seen Hope and Matthew alone together. Hope had said nothing had been going on between them and Levi didn't believe it.

"I'm fine. How's Hope and the other girls?"

"Hope is fine," Wilma said. "She's working at a bed and breakfast doing the cleaning."

"Yeah, I know about that. That's great, and how are the other girls?"

"All doing well."

"Would you like some pie? Surely you've got room for pie," Stephen said.

Matthew looked at everyone's dessert. "Well, just a small piece would be good."

Mercy stood. "I'll get you some."

"Thanks. And you're staying here a while?" Matthew looked at Wilma.

Levi filled him in on what they were doing and how long they planned to stay.

Wilma said, "I think you should know, Matthew, that a good friend of Hope's is joining the community."

"That's *wunderbaar*."

"A male friend," Jonathon told him, smirking.

"Oh, you mean …"

Wilma nodded.

Mercy put the plate of pie in front of him and then sat down. Matthew ate his pie in silence and as soon as he finished, he made excuses and left.

"That was a very abrupt exit," Levi said.

"It's understandable," Mercy said.

"Why?" Levi asked.

Wilma whispered, "I'll tell you later."

Mercy sat there not understanding how Levi didn't know that Matthew would be disappointed when he'd found out about Hope's friend.

After dessert, everyone sat in the living room drinking coffee and admiring the sleeping babies as they lay in their cribs.

"Look at them, you'd think they were twins," said Wilma.

"Only David's bigger," joked Jonathon, speaking about his son.

"*Nee,* Luke is," said Stephen. "And he was born first. So, he'll always be older than David."

"At least I'm older than you and always will be."

Mercy rolled her eyes. "The two of them could do this all day."

"What do you think about Fairfax, *Mamm.* Is he nice?" asked Honor.

"He's a lovely boy. We like him very much."

Levi added, "We do. We think that Hope and he will be perfect together."

"Just like me and Honor?" Jonathon said.

"Time will tell." Levi sipped his coffee.

That night Wilma and Levi were staying at Mercy's house and after they went to bed, Honor and Jonathon stayed longer to help Mercy clean up.

Honor and Mercy were alone in the kitchen and Honor was first to bring up the subject of Levi. "What do you feel now that you know Levi a little better?"

"He seems okay, but I can see what the girls say about him. He's very stubborn and persistent."

"That's not always a bad thing. I think he's okay."

"Well, he's not if he's going to try to stop *Mamm* from seeing Florence and the baby."

"I DON'T CARE what anyone says. I'll see Florence when I go back home to *Mamm's.*"

"Me too, I definitely will. I don't see the harm in it. If everyone turned their backs on her she'd never come back

to the community. It shows no love to cut people off."
Mercy sighed.

"There's two sides to that argument. The people who cut people off say that's their way of showing their love and that they're helping bring people back to the fold. Making them see that it's not alright by *Gott* to leave and mix in with the world and the worldly people."

"I don't think like that."

"Yeah, you and I think the same."

CHAPTER 20

ON SATURDAY MORNING, Hope called Mercy from the phone in the barn to find out if their mother had arrived safely. Mercy told her about the dinner they had the previous night with Levi and Wilma. She also told Hope that Matthew had appeared and asked about her extensively.

Hope had no doubt she would receive a long letter from Matthew asking her if there was any hope for him. It would be a difficult letter to write back, but she couldn't allow him to hold out any hope that something might happen between them. They'd never be a couple. There was a time when she thought Matthew would be the one she'd end up with if nobody else appeared for her.

She was so glad God had chosen Fairfax for her. It was almost a miracle since they'd been living beside one another all their lives and had never met. It was because their orchard was so large and the roads leading to their houses were different. Each had no need to even drive past the other's house.

~

THE GIRLS WERE busy all day Saturday, starting from sunup. Firstly, they cleaned the house, and then they decided that since the weather was nice they should have the dinner outside. A long table was carried out from the barn along with a gas grill. There were no chairs or benches, but they could carry all the kitchen and dining room chairs outside. There were sixteen chairs total.

Once that was done, they drove into the markets to buy the food. Then came the cooking.

By five in the afternoon, people were arriving.

When Bliss saw Adam, she wanted to be the first to speak to him. He stepped out of his buggy and secured the horse to the post.

"Hello, Adam," she said in a small voice.

He took a step toward her. "Hi, Bliss. Might I see your rabbit and her babies?"

"Of course. They're in my room. I'd love to show them to you."

"I would love to see them." He chuckled.

"Okay, let's go." Bliss walked up the stairs in front of him and swung open her bedroom door. It was the smallest bedroom in the house, but she didn't mind. She liked it that she could see nearly the entire apple orchard when she looked out of her window. It was a pleasant sight to wake up to every morning.

"Here you are, Bruiser. You don't mind if I call her Bruiser, do you?"

"That is a boy's name. She has a new name now."

"Okay, little bunny, to keep your mama happy I'll have

to call you by your new name, Cottonball." He lowered himself and picked up the rabbit. Bliss crouched down next to him and patted her rabbit while she was in his arms.

"She likes you."

"She remembers me, that's why."

"I think she does. And what do you think of her babies?"

He glanced down at the furry babies. "Cute. All babies are cute, especially baby rabbits."

Bliss covered her mouth and giggled. "Do you think that baby rabbits are as cute as baby people?"

"Of course. Especially the newborns, all wrinkly looking like old people."

Bliss smiled. "They're not all like that."

"I think we have a lot in common, Bliss."

"We do? Like what?"

"We both like animals and especially rabbits."

"That's true. What else would we have in common?"

He put Cottonball back in the hutch with the babies. "Why don't we find that out?"

Bliss liked the sound of that. "Okay"

"We can go on a buggy ride soon if you'd like."

"We are meeting on Tuesday. Remember?"

"I remember. That's all I've been thinking about. That, and tonight. I like what you said about Cherish in your letter."

Bliss couldn't remember what she'd said about Cherish.

"And she's your half-sister, right?"

"No. Stepsister."

"*Jah,* that's what I meant. She's your stepsister."

"I have so many sisters now and I already have two nephews and a niece. My niece is not in the community, but she only lives next door so I'm thinking we'll be seeing a lot of her."

"That's good. How would you like some practice?"

"Practice? Doing what?"

"Practice your new job. Hey, don't look at me like that. What did you think I was talking about?"

"Nothing. I wasn't thinking anything bad."

He laughed. "Don't worry about me, that's my sense of humor."

"Oh, I'll have to remember that. Practice making coffee you mean? Do you want me to make you a cup of coffee?"

"You've got it."

"Okay, I'd love to, except the machine at the cafe is very different from what we have here at home. We only have drip-filter coffee, using paper filters."

"That will be fine."

As they walked downstairs, she explained, "They have a big machine. They still have to show me how to use it. They said it takes many hours to get it just right."

"You're a smart girl. I reckon it would take you only half an hour."

"I hope so. I'm just pleased to have a job. Any sort of a job."

"Maybe I should have a coffee shop someday. I want my own business so I can work for myself."

"That would be a good idea except there are so many of them everywhere."

"That's because people have to eat and drink."

"And drink coffee," she said.

"That's right. It was a good idea having this barbecue. Whose idea was it?"

"Mine, and Cherish too. She thought it would be a good idea to have all the young people over here."

"I think it's a good idea too."

"And how do you think Fairfax is doing?"

"I think he's doing just fine. We're sharing quarters at the Millers.'"

"I know, that's why I asked."

"It's plenty big enough for two. We've had a few talks, but mostly he's asleep or working. So I don't get to see him all that much."

"Maybe men don't talk as much as women."

"I think they talk just as much."

When they got to the kitchen, she asked, "Do you have sugar and cream?"

"Yes, please, to both."

She put the teakettle on and then pulled one mug down from the high cupboard next to the sink.

"You're not having one?" he asked.

"No, I don't have any except at breakfast because it keeps me awake."

"Doesn't affect me one way or the other."

"That's good—if I could have one, I would."

As she made the coffee he asked, "So will this be the first job you had?"

"Yes, the first real job."

CHAPTER 21

CHERISH HAD SPENT her last cent on food for the barbecue. She had organized Favor and Hope to do the cooking and that left her free to talk with everyone, and have a good time, which was her favorite thing to do.

Hope was busy cooking, but Cherish figured she would abandon that when Fairfax arrived. He said he'd be there once all of his chores for the day were done.

When darkness blanketed the house, Cherish switched on the outside gas lighting.

Cherish stood on the porch watching everyone eating and having a good time. She wasn't going to let anyone in the house. No one was complaining. When she moved onto Dagmar's farm she intended to have many nights like this. Levi and *Mamm* always had the same old people for dinner. Cherish would invite everyone because it was lovely to watch so many people enjoying themselves.

When a car's headlights lit up the driveway coming toward the house, Cherish wasted no time moving inside out of the line of fire. She was convinced it was a hired car bringing Levi and *Mamm* back home—way ahead of schedule. They'd turned around and come home. Had they heard about the party?

When she saw another car following that one, she knew it was unlikely it was them. She walked back out of the house and waited to see what was going on.

A young woman stepped out of the first car. It was one of the girls she worked with from the café, Jainie. Cherish hurried over to greet her. She'd forgotten she'd invited her.

When she got close, she saw Jainie's eyes were glazed over and she could smell the alcohol. "Cherish! We're here to party," Jainie yelled out. A man who'd been driving the car joined her and he was holding two bottles. "I asked some friends. I hope that's okay."

Cherish nodded, not knowing what else to do or say.

The two men in the second car each carried a case of bottles. Judging by the way they were laughing and talking loudly, Cherish knew they were already drunk, too.

This wouldn't do. They'd have to go.

Hope walked over. "Cherish. Ask them to leave."

By now they'd sat down on the ground in a circle.

Cherish knew Hope was right. "Okay." She walked over. "Jainie, what are you doing? All of these people are drunk."

"You said it was a party and we've even brought our own drink."

"Not a party like that—not a party, party."

"That's what you said."

"It doesn't matter. You'll have to go and take all these people with you."

"Hey." One of the men jumped up. "That's not very hospicabell ... hospicable."

She knew what he was trying to say, but wasn't about to offer help. "I don't care. You'll have to go."

The young man pulled a cigarette out of his pocket, popped it in his mouth and lit it. He drew it in slowly and then blew smoke in Cherish's face. "We're not goin' nowhere."

"Relax, Cherish, nothing bad is going to happen. I thought you Amish were allowed to drink."

"Sometimes—some communities, but we don't get drunk."

"No one is forcing anyone, but we've got a car full. We brought plenty for everyone. We've got the trunk full of drinks."

In the pit of her stomach, Cherish just knew something more was going to go wrong. She turned around and walked away.

"Hey, is she gonna call the cops?" she heard one boy say to another when she walked away.

Cherish headed to Hope who was flipping over the hamburgers on the grill.

"Did you invite those men, Cherish?" Hope asked.

"No, they're friends of the girl I work with."

"All we need now is for the bishop to show up. This isn't good. We'll all be shunned and *Mamm* will not live for the shame."

"They can't do that to all of us, can they?"

"What's going on with them? They don't look friendly."

"I don't know. I'm too scared to ask them to leave again."

"We're not supposed to mix with outsiders and now you have some here at our house especially when our parents aren't here."

"Parent," Cherish said through gritted teeth, not wanting to think of Levi as her parent.

"I'll ask them to go," said Hope. Hope called a friend over to look after the food on the grill, and then she marched over to them. Meanwhile, Cherish wasted no time hurrying to the safety of the house.

Adam and Bliss walked over to the men and got there just before Hope. "What's the problem?" Adam asked.

"She invited us, and then told us to go."

"Well, if that's what she said, I think you should leave."

Another of the young men jumped up and walked up to Adam. "I don't care what ya think. We ain't goin' nowhere."

Bliss took hold of Adam's arm. "Come inside the house."

"Yes, you both should go inside," one of the men taunted him.

Bliss pulled him toward the house.

Once Adam and Bliss joined Cherish inside, she said, "How are we going to make them leave?"

"I don't know," said Bliss. "They seem aggressive, like they want to fight."

At that moment, two of the men barged in the house knocking everyone flying out of their way. One man had a full bottle of scotch in his hands. "Yous better not be callin' the cops."

"Not yet," Adam said. "Not if you leave peacefully."

She didn't want to even go near those boys to tell them to go home, and if they refused after her friends passed the message on, what could she do?

Hope walked in. "We have an outside bathroom if that's what you're looking for."

"Nah," said one of the men. "We just wanna warm ourselves by the fire."

"There is no fire," said Cherish. "It's not even cold enough for a fire right now. It might get cold enough tonight but it's certainly not cold enough now."

One man stood there and took off his T-shirt and handed it to the other man who poured scotch over it. Then he splashed some more of it around the room and on the curtains.

"Hey, stop it, you fool!" Cherish said.

"Get out," Adam called out, as he tried to grab the bottle. While he was busy wrestling the bottle out of one man's hands, the other man pulled out a lighter and lit the T-shirt. The shirt burst alight and then he threw it at the curtains and the place caught afire.

Cherish stood there barely believing what had just played out before her eyes. It was as though she was in a dream. *This can't be happening.* While the men ran out, Adam picked up the blanket from the back of the couch and started beating back the flames with it.

The girls ran to the kitchen to fill things up with water. When they came out to the living room again, the room was full of their friends smothering the flames. Fast thinking men had pulled burlap sacks from the barn. The flames were nearly out. Cherish looked around the room.

Where was Adam Wengerd?

CHAPTER 22

CHERISH STOOD there staring at the damage to the house in disbelief. Why had those young men thought it funny to damage her house? There was no reason for it. She ran outside when she heard shouting. The men hadn't driven off like Cherish thought they would've. They were still there and they were shouting at Adam. He was urging them to leave. One threw a punch at him and he threw his arm up to block it.

Cherish ran over. She didn't want a fight to take place. "I'll call the police if you don't leave now," Cherish yelled at the top of her lungs.

"You're so not cool," Jainie told her. "Let's go guys. This can't be the only party in town."

Without saying anything they got into their cars and drove away. One of the cars clipped the fence post on the way. Cherish didn't know if that was deliberate, but judging by the fire, she thought it might've been.

"Thank you, Adam. You were very brave."

"I don't think so. I just did what needed to be done."

Bliss joined them. "You *were* brave, Adam."

"Nah."

"Why did they do that?" Cherish sobbed suddenly from the shock of it all.

"They were drunk, Cherish." Bliss put a comforting arm around her shoulder.

"Yeah. They don't need a reason. Let's have a look at the damage. We'll have to have this fixed by the time your folks get back."

As they walked back inside, Cherish said, "The curtains are gone, the window frame's gone. It's all a huge mess and we've got no money to get it fixed before they get home."

"I'll fix it, don't worry. I've got loads of free time from now on." Adam looked over at Bliss and smiled. "I'll need a tape measure."

"Okay. We've got one that we use for dressmaking."

"That'll do."

They walked back into the house, passing their friends who were leaving. "No one called the fire department, did they?" Cherish asked. All was silent. That was a relief. If the volunteer fire department had been called out, there was no way they'd be able to keep it from Levi. Many of the firefighters were his friends.

The girls stood around and watched Adam take measurements. "I'll have this place fixed in no time."

"We can't tell anybody about this. No one. If *Mamm* and Levi find out they will never leave us alone again. And I'll get punished. They always blame me," Cherish said.

Adam nodded. "I can keep a secret."

"Bliss, why don't you go outside and tell everybody before they leave not to mention a word of this?"

"Okay." Bliss hurried out the door.

"We have no way of paying you. I spent all our money on food." Cherish looked around. "Anyone else have any money?"

"I have my weekly pay that I haven't given to Levi yet," said Hope.

"Give it to Adam and we'll find a way to pay it back to you."

Hope hurried to her room and brought back a handful of notes and gave them to Adam. He kept some and gave her back a hundred. "This is all I'll need. I'll borrow tools from the Millers. If one of you girls can bring me a sheet I'll nail it over the window. That'll keep insects out until I can get back here."

When they heard a buggy approaching the house, they all looked out the gaping hole where the window once was.

"It's Fairfax. Don't worry, I'll tell him not to mention a thing." Hope walked out of the house to see him while Cherish fetched Adam a hammer and nails.

"What's going on?" Fairfax asked when he met Hope.

"Drunk people came and set the house alight. It's okay now. Adam is going to do the repairs. The window frame's all gone, the curtains are gone and we'll have to re-paint the walls once they're fixed."

"Oh, that's dreadful. Are you okay?" He held Hope in his arms.

"I'm fine."

"Will you have to move out of the house?"

"*Nee*, the rest of the *haus* is all right. We'll have to get some curtain fabric from somewhere and it will have to be the same as what we had because … I don't want *Mamm* to ever learn what happened."

"Someone will tell her something."

"No. I'm telling everyone they can't say a word. I don't know why I was stupid enough to get roped into this idea."

Fairfax put his arm around her. "Don't worry about it. I'm sure they won't come back. They were just drunk."

"That doesn't matter, the crime has been committed."

"Forgive and forget. Isn't that what the bishop's always telling us?"

CHAPTER 23

CHERISH WALKED OUTSIDE to the food table to fix Adam something to eat.

"He offered to fix the place and that was so nice of him. We'll owe him something," Cherish told Favor.

"I'm sure he's happy to do it. And by the way he and Bliss are looking at one another I'm sure he'll be glad of any excuse to be around her."

Cherish had just taken a big bite of hamburger. She mumbled around it. "Bliss? What do you mean?"

"Well it's plain to see that they're fond of one another."

"I don't think so."

"*Jah,* they're *very* fond of one another, more accurately."

Cherish looked back at the house. "It's a little weird that he'd like Bliss."

"*Nee,* it's not. They both like rabbits."

Cherish swallowed her mouthful without chewing properly. Then she touched her throat and gulped as it had trouble going down. She wanted Adam to like her and now he liked Bliss because of that letter. "She never liked rabbits before I gave her one."

"Well, she likes 'em now. It was all in *Gott's* plan."

"It was my idea to give her the rabbit."

"*Jah*, in *Gott's* plan like I said."

"Okay, well … whatever." Cherish put the burger down. She'd lost her appetite.

They gathered up the leftover food and brought it into the house.

"I should get back to the Millers," Fairfax said. "I'm still not sure how to unhook a buggy. I've only driven one a few times so far. It might take a while and I've got an early start tomorrow."

The girls giggled at him talking about unhooking a buggy.

"There's nothing to it." Adam kindly kept a straight face. "I'll follow you and then we can do it together and I'll show you what to do."

"The Millers must have a lot of buggies since you're both using borrowed ones," Cherish said.

"They only have the two, but they weren't using them today," Adam said. "Lucky for me."

Fairfax and Hope walked out the door first and Adam stayed behind giving them a quiet moment to say their goodbyes.

"Don't worry girls, I'll be back as soon as I get the wood from the lumberyard and then I'll start work. I'll borrow the Millers' tools."

"Don't worry, we have plenty of tools," Bliss said. "We've got Mr. Baker's tools and my *Dat's* too."

"Okay, good, but I'll bring some spares just in case. Now don't you girls worry, and no one get stressed about this. You'll have a working window by tomorrow evening."

"Wait. Tomorrow is Sunday," Cherish said.

Adam rubbed his head. "It is, you're right. I've lost track of the days. That means I'll get started first thing Monday."

All the girls thanked him. When every one of their guests was gone, the four girls sat down staring at one another.

"I'm sorry, all right," Cherish blurted out.

"It's not your fault," Bliss said. "We all agreed to have the BBQ. No one could know what was going to happen. Besides, it was my stupid idea to begin with."

"Yes," Cherish said dejectedly, "but it was my idea that it would be okay to invite Jainie. At work, she always seemed mature and responsible. I never expected all of this." She waved a hand around to take in the chaos.

Hope stared at the curtains. "Well, those curtains are the same as the curtains in the kitchen. I'll go on Monday and see if I can get the same fabric."

"Yeah, but what are you going to pay with?" Favor asked. "I've given all our money to Adam for the lumber."

"We've still got one hundred from my pay, remember? He said he didn't need all of it. The fabric will be much less than that. Then we'll need paint. Do we have anything we could sell?" suggested Hope.

"Now that Levi's gone we could set up a roadside stall."

"If we spend all day tomorrow praying for a solution rather than working, God can work miracles," Bliss said.

"That's true," said Cherish, just to keep everyone happy. What she truly believed was that God didn't help people who sat around praying while doing nothing.

Bliss sighed. "I'm so silly."

"We all went along with it," said Favor. "That makes us all at fault."

"You're right, Favor. It's at times like these we need each other and it doesn't matter if one or two of us have made a mistake, we're all in this together as sisters. Whatever hardships we face, we'll face them together."

Cherish put her arm around Bliss. She wasn't too bad —sometimes.

"Well, I'm going to bed," said Hope as she jumped to her feet.

Favor sniggered. "Go to bed and think about your boyfriend."

"That's right. I'm not going to bed to think about this." She pointed at the sheet-covered wall that was once a window.

While Hope marched up the stairs the other three stared at one another.

Maybe, Cherish thought, she was being punished for having a party without adults being there ... but Adam had been there and he was in his twenties. So, there technically *had* been an adult there. If all went well, *Mamm* and Levi might decide to extend their stay. That would give them time to fix this mess.

CHAPTER 24

ON SUNDAY, because it was the day of rest, they didn't need to cook a big breakfast like they usually had. The minimum work was always done on Sundays, and that included the cooking. Cherish decided to make everybody toast with jam, or toast with marmalade, or with peanut butter, or—totally boring, she thought—with plain old butter.

With six slices of bread under the griller, she placed the teakettle on the stove.

"I hope that nobody that was there last night talks about what happened here. We'll have to get around to everybody again and tell them not to mention a thing. The last thing I want is for this to get back to Levi."

"That's right, Cherish," said Bliss, agreeing. "We'll get around to visit everybody and tell them not to mention anything."

"Agreed, you two?" Cherish looked at Hope and Favor who were sitting down at the kitchen table.

"Of course we agree," said Favor. "Hope can't think about anything else except seeing her boyfriend."

The girls laughed, and Hope didn't seem to mind.

"How's he doing with the Millers?" Cherish asked.

"All right as far as I know. Why, what have you heard?"

Cherish threw her hands in the air. "Nothing. Why is everybody so defensive all the time?"

"I'm not. I'm just wondering if you've heard anything." Hope nibbled on a fingernail.

"*Nee*, is there anything to hear? Is he changing his mind?"

"Don't even say that. Don't even *think* that."

"I wouldn't have thought that if you hadn't said what you said just now."

Bliss said. "We should visit Adam and make sure he doesn't forget to fix the window tomorrow like he said he would. If he changes his mind, we'll have to find someone else to do it. Then we'll run out of time."

"Okay," Cherish said knowing Hope wanted to see Fairfax again. It was also a way of her seeing Adam again. She didn't get much of a chance to see him with Bliss talking to him all the time.

"I'm sure Fairfax could help him with the repairs too. He does get a break in the middle of the day."

"I'll talk to Adam about it," said Bliss.

"Better still, I'll talk to him," Cherish said.

"Okay, suits me. Whoever sees him first will talk to him," said Bliss.

"Do you realize this is the first Sunday we've ever had in this *haus* without *Mamm?*" Favor said. "This is the first time she's left us alone."

Cherish took the kettle off the stove "Who's having tea and who's having *kaffe?*"

"*Kaffe* for me please," said Bliss

"And for me," said Hope raising her hand.

"Me too please, if it's not too much trouble, Cherish."

"It is a bit of trouble. Why don't you do the *kaffes*, Favor? Then I'll spread the toast."

Cherish spread the toast with an assortment of toppings and placed the plate in the center of the table.

"I feel like peanut butter," said Bliss. "It was a bad thing that happened to the house, but it's good because I'll see more of Adam when he comes to fix the window."

"Oh, so you like him and you admit it?" Cherish asked.

"I do." Bliss took a large bite of her peanut butter toast.

"Do you remember when I saw him at the mud sale? I pointed at him and I said, He's mine.'"

Bliss raised her eyebrows and finished her mouthful. "You don't like him, Cherish. He said things to you and you told me you didn't like him. You were pleased when he left, but now he's back."

"I like him again now. Besides, he apologized and admitted he was wrong. I like the way he got rid of those men who were behaving dreadfully."

"Behaving dreadfully? They were *awful*."

"And Adam acted very brave and masterfully. I like men like that. I like to have someone I can look up to."

Bliss's bottom lip trembled, just like one of her rabbits' noses. "You've got nothing in common with him, though."

"And what would you have in common with a man like that?"

"Rabbits. We both like rabbits."

"I was the one who got the rabbit so I like them the most. It was all my idea at the start and I put dibs on him."

"Stop it you two. This is nonsense. It's not good to argue like this. Cherish, you're the youngest. Bliss is older so let her have him," Hope said.

"That's hardly fair."

"Of course it is. You like a different man every week so what's the difference? And who has Bliss ever liked? No one."

"He's the first man I've ever liked and the only one," said Bliss in a quiet voice

"You can have him. Unless…"

Bliss leaned forward. "Unless what?"

"Unless he likes me better."

"That sounds fair enough to me," said Favor.

"Just don't entice him like you've enticed other men in the past," Hope told her.

"I won't do anything at all. I won't have to."

Bliss leaned forward and patted Cherish's arm. *"Denke."*

Cherish couldn't believe that Bliss thought the whole thing was over and done with. It was unbelievable that Bliss might think that Adam liked her better.

"Okay Bliss, you talk to Adam today as long as I can talk to him tomorrow when he gets here—without anyone listening. I'll meet him as soon as he gets out of the buggy. Okay?"

"You're not coming with us today?" asked Bliss.

"*Nee.* I'm so upset I need to calm down and be by myself."

"I hope I haven't upset you."

Hope put her arm around Bliss. "You didn't. It's just the situation."

"Well, what do you say?" asked Cherish.

"*Jah,* it's fine. Whatever you want."

CHAPTER 25

WHEN THE GIRLS LEFT, tears started flowing down Cherish's face. It hurt her that Hope had said she should let Bliss have Adam just because Bliss was older. Didn't Hope care about her? She felt so alone. She walked outside and called for Caramel. He came bounding toward her. She sat on the porch steps cuddling him. That made her feel better.

Then she realized what would make her feel even better was to talk to Florence. She'd give her advice about the situation. Bliss wasn't so much older than she was and surely it was Adam's decision which one of them he liked. They couldn't decide between them who should have him. Florence would agree with her.

"Inside, Caramel." Caramel looked up at her. "Nee, you can't come. I'm going to visit Florence and if you come you'll be in the way." She opened the door and took Caramel to the couch. He jumped up. "Stay there and be a good boy until I get back."

Once he was settled, Cherish left him, wiped her eyes

and set off through the orchard to Florence and Carter's house.

When she got to their door she realized the baby might be asleep so she knocked quietly.

Carter opened the door. "Hi, Cherish." Before she could respond he took a better look. "What's wrong?"

"Nothing ... Everything."

"Come in."

"Oh, is it a bad time? Is the baby asleep?"

"No. Florence has just fed her. They're in the living room." He opened the door wide and she walked through.

"Thanks."

"Looks like I'm not needed. I'll be upstairs."

No one responded to Carter, so he slipped up the stairs while Cherish sat next to Florence. Cherish smiled at the baby and touched her arm. "Hello, *boppli.*"

"What's wrong?" Florence asked.

"I'm sorry to come here like this but there's no one else I can talk to. No one understands me."

"What's happened?"

"You see there's this man."

"Ah, I thought it might be over a man."

Cherish told Florence what had happened, about the damage to the house, and then she took a deep breath and told her the whole truth of what happened and about the fake letter. "So you see, he really likes me and not Bliss. He liked the person who wrote the letter. What should I do?"

"I think you should confess what you've done—to both of them and say you're sorry."

"I couldn't."

"The truth will come out and everyone will think less of you. If you confess, that allows you to save face."

Cherish thought for a moment. The only reason she wrote that letter was that she truly thought she'd never see Adam Wengerd ever again. "I guess you're right. Now that he's come back, that's changed everything. And if I tell the truth then he'll also know that I wrote the letter. He might forgive me and then we can be a couple."

"Don't be upset if that doesn't happen. What you did was deceptive and I can't even believe that you did it." Florence shook her head. "Put yourself in his position. If that had happened to you, how would you feel about that person?"

"I might think it's funny."

"No! It's not funny, Cherish. It's not funny at all. Letters shouldn't be tampered with. Letters are personal communication between one person and another."

"*Jah*, I know. It was bad of me. I shouldn't have done it. You're right. I'll confess what I've done and take the consequences, whatever they might be."

"Good. And please, don't ever do anything like that again. It doesn't lead down a good path."

Cherish smiled at her big sister. "I know. I've learned that the hard way."

"Good. I'm glad you've learned it. It took you long enough."

"Do you think I could hold my niece?"

"Sure. Maybe you could rock her to sleep."

"I can try." Cherish stood and then leaned down and took baby Iris from Florence. Then she walked around patting her on the back until she fell asleep.

Ten minutes later, Cherish headed back home and spent the rest of the afternoon rehearsing what she'd say to Bliss and Adam. She'd tell Adam first because she couldn't risk Adam learning the news from Bliss. No. She had to be the one to tell Adam, with her own mouth. She spent the rest of Sunday thinking exactly what she would say in her confession.

ADAM ARRIVED in a wagon just after nine the next morning. Cherish said to all the girls who were in the kitchen. "You all better stay here while I talk to Adam for a minute. Okay?"

When the girls agreed, Cherish walked out of the house. She could see from the timber in the back of the wagon that he'd already gotten the supplies he needed for the window. "Adam, I have to talk with you."

He grinned at her. "What is it?"

"I have a confession to make."

"Are you sure you're talking to the right person?" He seemed a little concerned.

She smiled and stepped closer. "I wrote that letter to you. It wasn't from Bliss at all."

His eyebrows drew together. "What letter was that?"

"I don't know. How many letters did Bliss send you?"

"Just the one." He was silent for a moment as he searched her face. "Wait a minute. You wrote that letter to me saying I should apologize to you and you pretended the letter was from Bliss?"

"That's right."

"Did Bliss know about this?"

"*Nee*. She wrote a different letter to you." Cherish bit her lip, hoping for a good outcome.

"Hmm. And what happened to that one?"

"I substituted it with my letter."

He shook his head. "Why would you do that?"

She inhaled deeply when she saw he was upset. "It seemed like a good idea at the time." With trembling fingers, she straightened her prayer *kapp*.

He moved to the back of the wagon and pulled out the wooden toolbox. "If you'll excuse me I've got some work to do."

Her mouth fell open. She knew for a fact he told Bliss he liked her letter, so why was he acting like that? "Wait up." Cherish hurried after him.

He stopped and turned to her. "I can't believe you'd do such a thing and then tell me about it as though I'd be pleased."

"You said how rude you were to me and you apologized, so aren't we even?" Her eyelashes fluttered and she gave her best smile with her head slightly to one side. That cuteness normally worked with men.

"No. We're nowhere near even. 'Even' has nothing to do with it. You deceived me and you deceived your sister, and that's worse. How could you do that to her?"

"You told her you liked her because of the letter, but don't you see ... I was the one who wrote it?" From the fact that she had to explain that last bit, she knew things weren't working in her favor.

He shook his head at her. "You'll have to tell Bliss what you've done."

Cherish's eyes grew wide. "I will. I planned to as soon as I told you." She had to know … "You still like her?"

"Of course I do. She's sweet and kind."

"Yeah, but I thought you liked a different kind of girl."

"No!" He turned and kept walking toward the house.

Cherish sat down right where she was—on the ground —defeated. Adam was clearly a man who didn't know what he wanted and why was she surprised? A man who tricked people when he sold rabbits was never going to suit her. She picked up a nearby pebble and tossed it as far as she could. Then she did the same with another, and then another.

NOT LONG AFTER Fairfax arrived at the house to help with the repairs, Hope arrived, driven by her boss, Fairfax's aunt.

Hope jumped out of the car with a quick word of thanks, and hurried to the house. She'd been given the rest of the day off after she explained the situation to her boss.

"I'M SO pleased to see you could make it," Fairfax said to her as soon as she walked into the house.

"Me too. Your Aunt Jane is a wonderful woman."

He walked over to her and whispered, "Maybe we'll have time to talk after I help Adam fix this window."

"I hope so, but first I need to take one of the girls into town with me to get fabric for the curtain."

Fairfax whispered to her, "Take Bliss or Cherish, but

not both. I don't know what's gone on, but they're not happy with each other."

"Oh, I'll take Cherish, then. She'll tell me what's happening."

Along with a piece of what was left of one of the curtains, Hope took Cherish into town to get the new fabric. On the way, she learned what happened about the letter. Bliss had been very upset when Cherish had told her what she'd done.

Cherish went on to tell Hope, "They say it's good to be honest, but no one's happy about me telling the truth."

"It's not that, Cherish. You know you were wrong. It's good that you apologized to them both but I think they need time to breathe, time to process it. What you did was unthinkable. I can hardly believe it."

"Oh, don't say that. It makes me feel worse."

"Maybe you *should* feel worse so you won't do it again."

"I won't. Trust me." When they got to the fabric store, Cherish was too upset to go in with Hope so she waited in the buggy. If only she hadn't sent that letter. It wouldn't have been a problem if Adam Wengerd had just stayed away.

When they got home, they saw the window frame had been replaced. Now all they needed was a glazier to finish the job off.

"That's all we can do today. That has to cure a little, then I'll finish with the window tomorrow."

"How long is this going to take to finish completely?" Favor asked staring at the window.

"It takes as long as it will take. I'll make some calls to

find a good glazier and we should have everything done and painted before your folks come back. I've already tried to match the paint and they don't have anything that matches exactly."

"The paint doesn't have to match exactly. As long as it's close we can paint the whole room."

"Okay. I'll head off now and get the paint," Fairfax said.

Hope smiled. "I'll come with you."

Cherish walked past everyone and headed up the stairs not saying a word.

No sooner had she closed the door and sat on her bed than Bliss walked in and closed the door behind her. "I forgive you."

Cherish was taken aback. Normally she would've said something smart-mouthed, but this time she didn't want to. "*Denke*. I do realize what an awful thing I did. Adam doesn't even like me, he likes you even though I wrote the stupid letter that he said he liked." Cherish sighed.

"He and I've gotten to know each other. That's why." She sat on the edge of Cherish's bed.

"Why have you forgiven me so fast?"

"We're *schweschders* and besides that, you got me that job. I start tomorrow and I'm so excited."

"*Denke*." Cherish leaned over and hugged Bliss as a tear trickled down her cheek. In that moment, Cherish truly was sorry.

CHAPTER 26

BLISS'S STOMACH churned as she pushed the door of the cafe and walked inside on the first day of her first real job. Her nerves lessened when she saw Rocky's smiling face from behind the counter. He gave her a wave and walked toward her with his hand outstretched.

"Welcome to our crew, Bliss."

"Thank you for giving me the work."

"You come highly recommended. Cherish is one of our best workers."

Bliss was a little surprised about that. She thought it was Cherish's personality that got her by. "Well, I hope I can be just as good a worker as she is."

"I'm sure you will be. Before you go today, I'll have you fill out some paperwork. Right now, let's get you started learning how to make coffees."

"Okay."

He took her behind the counter where she met a woman in her thirties with large black glasses and dark hair pulled back tightly into a high ponytail.

"This is Debbie. One of our supervisors."

"Pleased to meet you. Bliss, isn't it?"

"That's right. And I'm happy to meet you, too." Bliss hoped she wouldn't see Jainie, the girl who'd been at their place the other night.

"Did you bring a bag or anything?" Debbie asked.

"No, I just bought myself."

"I'll leave you with Debbie," Rocky told her.

"Yes, I'll look after her." Debbie then proceeded to show her, step by step, how to make coffee, making one for herself in the process. "Now, you have a go and see if you remember."

With a metal implement, Bliss pushed the ground coffee down into the round metal container.

"And a bit more. We like to have our coffee fairly strong. That's what the customers are used to."

She added some more, and looked at Debbie for confirmation.

"That's the way. Then what?"

"I put it in here and press the button."

"Good. Then we froth the milk. Here, you have a go at that, too. It's easy with this machine. It practically does it by itself."

They watched for a moment while the machine worked its magic. Then Bliss poured the foamy milk into the coffee, even making a swirly pattern like Debbie had just done.

"Perfect. Now shake a few sprinkles on top. Then drink it, and see what you think."

Bliss giggled. "Okay." She had a sip. "Nice."

"I think you'll work out well."

"I hope so. What do I have to know about taking orders and things like that?"

Debbie gave her a full rundown of the procedures. Time flew by and it seemed in no time it was two o'clock.

Rocky appeared from the back room. "Home time for you, Bliss. Have you filled out that paperwork?"

"No. I'll do that now."

While she was filling out the paperwork on the back counter, he asked, "Same time next week?"

"Yes, I'd love that."

"Good. I should be able to give you and Cherish some more hours. Jainie called in sick, for the umpteenth time, this week. We had to let her go."

"That's too bad for her, but that would suit me just fine."

"Debbie told me you did a good job today."

"I hope so." She'd been told they hadn't had a busy day and Tuesdays were like that sometimes. But she was disappointed that she hadn't made any tips. Maybe the customers didn't like her as much as they liked Cherish.

When she walked out the door, she saw Adam leaning against a buggy. She hurried over to him and then he saw her and walked a few steps towards her. "How was your first day?"

"Really good. I loved it and they're going to keep me on and give me more work too."

"That's good to hear. It makes a difference if you like your job. Do you have to go straight home?"

"No. I can be home any time. What did you have in mind?"

"I didn't have anything in mind really. What is there to see around here?"

"I'll take you to my favorite place ever."

He chuckled. "And what's that?"

"It's the river."

"Oh," he said with a surprised look. "I thought it was going to be some kind of a store."

"Oh no. This is the place I always used to go whenever anyone upset me. It always makes me feel better."

"Okay, jump in."

Soon, they were walking along the riverbank, and Bliss couldn't keep the smile from her face. He certainly was handsome, but it still worried her that he wore his hat tipped back and she didn't know why. Didn't he see that no one in the community here wore his hat like that? It was something that didn't matter, but could she see past it? Would he be upset if she said something?

"I'm glad I came to visit your community because if I hadn't I never would've met you."

She looked up at his smiling face. "I'm glad too."

"And we have got your sister to thank for us getting to know each other better."

"Because of Bruiser?"

He laughed. "Because of Cottonball."

"Yes."

"Do you want to breed her again?"

"No. I haven't even found homes for the four that she has. I'd like to keep them all, but…"

"But your mother would kill you, I know."

"That's right. Anyway, Cottonball's a pet. I always wanted a pet and I thought I wanted a dog, but not anymore. I couldn't imagine having anything other than a rabbit."

"I know. I feel the same.

"I think they're the best pets ever."

He laughed. "Me too."

She reached up and straightened his hat. "There. That's better."

"That's how you like it?"

"It is."

"Then that's how I'll always wear it." They stared into each other's eyes. He then leaned forward until their lips nearly touched.

Bliss got scared and backed away. "How's the window coming along today?" she asked as she kept walking.

"All done. The glass has been fitted and it looks great. Favor and Cherish are painting and Hope's nearly got the curtain finished.

"That's good. I'm so relieved. It's all my fault. The dinner was my idea."

"It's not your fault at all, Bliss." He stopped and gently touched her arm, so she stopped walking too. "What would you think if I moved here for good?"

Bliss stopped breathing for a moment. This was perfect. She didn't want to move away anywhere and if he was willing to move here, what could be better? "You'd do that?"

"I would for you."

She couldn't stop the smile that tugged at her lips. He leaned down and she tilted her face upward and soon their lips touched. Then he gently put his arm around her waist and pulled her toward him. She pulled back from the kiss and leaned her head against his shoulder and put her arms around him. They held each other for ages before he whispered, "I'm going to make arrangements to move here right away."

"I'd like that," she whispered back.

CHAPTER 27

ONE WEEK LATER, Wilma and Levi arrived home.

Wilma sat down heavily on the couch after the girls all greeted her with excited hugs. "I can't even tell you how good it is to be home. I feel like I've been traveling for months."

"Did you miss us, *Mamm?*" Cherish asked, sitting on the rug at *Mamm's* feet.

"*Jah*, I did. I missed each and every one of you girls, but now that I'm here I miss my two oldest and their babies."

"They can visit us," Bliss said. "I can't wait to see them again."

"I can't wait to see them either," said Cherish not wanting to be outdone by her stepsister. "We haven't even seen the *bopplis*, not even once."

"Something's different." *Mamm* looked around.

"Like what?" Favor sat on the floor next to Cherish and the other girls sat on the end of the couch on the other side of Levi.

Mamm had a good look around, swiveling her head this way and that. "The curtains."

Cherish jumped up and took hold of the curtains in her hands. "We all made new curtains as a surprise."

"Why did you do that? There was nothing wrong with the old ones."

"They were a bit …" Cherish hesitated to lie. It had already landed her in enough trouble.

"*Nee,* Cherish. It was me, *Mamm.*"

Levi said, "What did you do, Bliss?"

"It was Cottonball."

Mamm shook her head. "I told you that rabbit would ruin the *haus.*" *Mamm's* glare transferred from Bliss to Cherish.

"It's not Cherish's fault, *Mamm.* If anyone should get into trouble it should be me."

"Well, I can't get mad at you since you confessed and you made things right."

"*Denke, Mamm.*" Bliss looked over at Cherish who gave her a smile back.

Wilma wasn't done yet. "And is it my eyes, or is the color of the walls different?"

"Nothing's changed," said Cherish, before she had time to think it through. "It might be because you've come in from the brightness of the sun."

Favor said, "Or it might be that the curtains are a slightly different color and that makes the walls different."

"That could be it," said *Mamm.*

"We've made the evening meal. I know it's too early, but you can have it now if you're hungry," Bliss said.

Mamm sniffed the air. "It's a tiny bit smoky. I hope

that's rabbit stew," *Mamm* said with a laugh. "I can smell smoke, so is it smoked rabbit?"

Bliss's mouth turned down at the corners and her eyes went wide.

"Mamm's only joking. We'll never eat rabbit in this *haus* again," Favor said, patting Bliss's shoulder.

"Not unless it's one particular rabbit," *Mamm* said.

"It's just *Mamm's* sense of humor. Don't worry, Cotton-wool's quite safe," said Cherish.

"It's Cottonball," said Bliss quietly.

"Cottonball today, but it might be Cottonwool tomor-row," said *Mamm*. All the girls giggled at Wilma. "Speaking of names, what did Florence end up calling her baby?"

"She called her Iris," said Bliss, before the Baker girls could break it to their mother gently. After all, Iris was her late sister's name and she was so emotional every time she spoke of Iris.

"Iris," *Mamm* repeated, a hand going to her chest as though it had a mind of its own. "Well, that makes me ..." The girls held their breath. "That makes me very happy. Iris should be remembered by us, and by Carter. What a lovely way to do that."

FLORENCE STARED out her window at the tiny trees that had been planted. Now she had something to watch grow alongside her little girl, and that felt so satisfying. Only a quarter of the space they had was planted, but it was a start. Everything was coming together. She closed her eyes and said a prayer of thanks for the wonderful life that was now hers. Only a few years before everything seemed so futile and hopeless.

All she needed now was to get some sleep. Carter was taking his turn caring for Iris upstairs while he was looking over preliminary plans for their new house. Florence had a moment to herself to relax. All she could think about was next door. Had Wilma and Levi returned? She recalled what Cherish had told her about the damage to the house. What did Levi and Wilma think about the work on the house, or, had they even noticed that anything was different?

She was still holding on to the hope that one day, in God's timing, the Bakers Apple Orchard would land in her lap. It was always meant to be hers. She knew it in her heart.

Thank you for reading Amish Bliss.

www.SamanthaPriceAuthor.com
samantha@samanthapriceauthor.com

THE NEXT BOOK IN THE SERIES

What's in store for the Baker girls and the apple orchard?
Find out in: Book 11 Amish Apple Harvest
Favor is tired of being overlooked and ignored, so she
does something that shocks everyone.
Will Cherish make the right decision when she learns the
success of the harvest is in her hands? How will this
impact Florence's goals to gain back control of the
orchard?

THE AMISH BONNET SISTERS

Book 1 Amish Mercy

Book 2 Amish Honor

Book 3 A Simple Kiss

Book 4 Amish Joy

Book 5 Amish Family Secrets

Book 6 The Englisher

Book 7 Missing Florence

Book 8 Their Amish Stepfather

Book 9 A Baby For Florence.

Book 10 Amish Bliss

ALL SAMANTHA PRICE BOOK SERIES

Amish Maids Trilogy
A 3 book Amish romance series of novels featuring 5 friends finding love.

Amish Love Blooms
A 6 book Amish romance series of novels about four sisters and their cousins.

Amish Misfits
A series of 7 stand-alone books about people who have never fitted in.

The Amish Bonnet Sisters
To date there are 28 books in this continuing family saga. My most popular and best-selling series.

Amish Women of Pleasant Valley
An 8 book Amish romance series with the same characters. This has been one of my most popular series.

Ettie Smith Amish Mysteries
An ongoing cozy mystery series with octogenarian sleuths. Popular with lovers of mysteries such as Miss Marple or Murder She Wrote.

Amish Secret Widows' Society
A ten novella mystery/romance series - a prequel to the Ettie Smith Amish Mysteries.

Expectant Amish Widows
A stand-alone Amish romance series of 19 books.

Seven Amish Bachelors
A 7 book Amish Romance series following the Fuller brothers' journey to finding love.

Amish Foster Girls
A 4 book Amish romance series with the same characters who have been fostered to an Amish family.

Amish Brides
An Amish historical romance. 5 book series with the same characters who have arrived in America to start their new life.

Amish Romance Secrets
The first series I ever wrote. 6 novellas following the same characters.

Amish Christmas Books

Each year I write an Amish Christmas stand-alone romance novel.

Amish Twin Hearts
A 4 book Amish Romance featuring twins and their friends.

Amish Wedding Season
The second series I wrote. It has the same characters throughout the 5 books.

Amish Baby Collection
Sweet Amish Romance series of 6 stand-alone novellas.

Gretel Koch Jewel Thief
A clean 5 book suspense/mystery series about a jewel thief who has agreed to consult with the FBI.

Made in United States
Cleveland, OH
09 February 2025